A BOOK OF THE
LOVE OF JESUS

From the painting by Velasquez

PRINTED BY SIR ISAAC PITMAN & SONS, LTD.,
ENGLAND

TO JESUS CHRIST
GOD AND MAN TO ALL HIS TRUE LOWERS

PREFACE

THIS book is an attempt to present some devotions of our forefathers in a form which it would be possible for modern Christian? to use. The difficulty, of course, has been in deciding how far the archaic words and phrases were to be retained, and how far rendered by modern equivalents : and I fully expect to be criticised from either side ; on the one hand by those who say that it is perhaps a profanity, and certainly an error of taste, to tamper at all with the old vocabulary; and on the other hand by those who say that an archaic flavour, however slight, hinders the free reality and the natural flow of their devotion. I hasten co express my confidence that in many instances strictures will be only too well deserved ; and yet I deprecate sweeping condemnation partly on the grounds ot the real difficulty of the task, and of my own good intentions ; and still more on the ground

that in questions of this kind definite canons cannot be followed to the exclusion of individual requirement and taste. For it has been my deliberate object to adapt the devotions for those who would be incapable of praying in, and per haps even of understanding, the old English in which they were written. It seemed a pity that modern Christians should be deprived of these spiritual treasures merely because they were un able to appreciate their original literary form. The utmost that I have done, too, even in extreme instances (which are few), is to melt down the old coin and re-issue it in a more current mould. This, superficially, may be ress romantic, but it is more practical, than to let these treasures rust unknown except to a few scholars. And, after all, the original composers wrote down their devotions, we may suppose, for the spiritual use, and not for the antiquarian ad miration, of the generauons that should follow them.

As regards the adaptation of the poetry, the difficulty has been especially great in deciding between the often conflicting claims of the rhyme, the rhythm, the sense, and the intelligibility. Nor have I always been consistent in my attempts at arbitration. Sometimes I have

viii

sacrificed the one, and sometimes the other: occasionally I have replaced some archaic word or phrase by its modern equivalent; while in other places, where its meaning was obviously indicated by the context, I have allowed it to stand. It has been found impossible, too, always to preserve the sequences of alliterative words, which are so marked a characteristic of Richard Rolle's writings ; and I have scarcely even at tempted to retain the actual semi-rhythmical lines that occur here and there in his prose-medi tations.

As regards the debt that I owe to the volumes that have been the sources of this book, it is im possible to say more than that, for the greater part, they have been its sources. But perhaps I need not do more here than refer the reader to the Notes, which will direct him to these books, where he may find the devotions in their original form.

The first set of prayers before and after Com munion I owe to a transcript made by the Rev. Walter Frere, of the Community of the Resur rection, from a Lambeth MS. ; at whose sug gestion, indeed, the work was begun, and from whose help and sympathy during its progress I have gained so much.

Preface]

(Perhaps, too, in this connection, it is right to add that the book was practically finished while I was still a member of the Church of England.)

Briefly then ; the book is published as a con tribution, not to antiquarian study, but to de votional life. And it will be found, I believe, that these exquisite verses and meditations will especially afford fruitful material and inspiration for mental prayer, as well as forms for vocal com munion with God.

Robert Hugh Benson AFSC KC*SG KGCHS (18 November 1871 – 19 October 1914) was an English Anglican priest who in 1903 was received into the Roman Catholic Church in which he was ordained priest in 1904. He was a prolific writer of fiction and wrote the notable dystopian novel Lord of the World (1907). His output encompassed historical, horror and science fiction, contemporary fiction, children's stories, plays, apologetics, devotional works and articles. He continued his writing career at the same time as he progressed through the hierarchy to become a Chamberlain to the Pope in 1911 and subsequently titled Monsignor.

Early life: Benson was the youngest son of Edward White Benson (Archbishop of Canterbury) and his wife, Mary, and the younger brother of Edward Frederic Benson and A. C. Benson. Benson was educated at Eton College and then studied classics and theology at Trinity College, Cambridge, from 1890 to 1893.

In 1895, Benson was ordained a priest in the Church of England by his father, who was the then Archbishop of Canterbury.

Career: After his father died suddenly in 1896, Benson was sent on a trip to the Middle East to recover his own health. While there he began to question the status of the Church of England and to consider the claims of the Roman Catholic Church. His own piety began to tend toward the High Church tradition, and he started exploring religious life in various Anglican communities, eventually obtaining permission to join the Community of the Resurrection.

Benson made his profession as a member of the community in 1901, at which time he had no thoughts of leaving the Church of England. As he continued his studies and began writing, however, he became more and more uneasy with his own doctrinal position and, on 11 September 1903, he was received into the Catholic Church. He was awarded the Dignitary of Honour of the Order of the Holy Sepulchre.

Benson was ordained as a Roman Catholic priest in 1904 and sent to Cambridge. He continued his writing career along with his ministry as a priest.

Novelist: Like both his brothers, Edward Frederic Benson ("Fred") and Arthur Christopher Benson, Robert wrote many ghost and horror stories, as well as children's stories and historical fiction. His horror and ghost fiction are collected in The Light Invisible (1903) and A Mirror of Shallott (1907). His novel, Lord of the World (1907), is generally regarded as one of the first modern dystopian novels (see List of dystopian literature). The bibliography below reveals a prodigious output.

CONTENTS

	Page
CHARACTERISTICS OF ENGLISH DEVOTIONS . .	xv

The Devotions

AN INTRODUCTION TO PRAYER . . . 1

PART I

THE LOVE OF JESUS:
1. A Song of the Love of Jesus. *Jesus, who might thy sweetness see* . . 7
2. Richard de Castre's Prayer to Jesus. *Jesu, Lord, that madest me* . . 12
3. The Virtues of the Name Jesus . . 15
4. The Love of Jesus. *Love is life that lasteth aye* 21
5. A Loving Song to Jesus. *Jesu Christ, saint Mary's Son* . . . 27
6. The Comfort of Christ Jesus. *So be my comfort, Christ Jesus* . . 31
7. Short Songs to Jesus:
    (i) *Jesu, as thou me made* . . 35
    (ii) *Jesu Christ, God's Son* . . 35

Contents]

THE LOVE OF JESUS — continued
Page
(iii) Jesu, at thy will 36
(iv) Jesu, since thou canst do thy will 36
(v) Jesu Christ^ have mercy . . 37
(vi) In world oj worlds . . . 37
(vii) Jesu mine 38
8. Two Prayers to Jesus :
(i) A Good Prayer to Jesus . . 39
(ii) A Prayer for Grace and Glory . 41

PART II
THE PASSION OF JESUS :
1. An Introduction to the Passion : and
R. Rolle's Meditation ... 45
2. A Song to Jesus and Mary in the Passion.
Sweet Jesu, now will I sing . . 72
3. A Meditation of the Five Wounds. . 82
4. A Devotion on the Symbols of the
Passion. O vernacle . * . . 87
5. The Example of the Passion. Set what
our Lord suffered . . . -,. 101
6. A Meditation on the Passion, and on
Three Arrows of Doomsday . . 105
7. Cantus Christi :
(i) Unkind man 118
(ii) Sinful man . . . . ,120
(iii) Lo sweet beloved . . . 120

xii
[Contents

PART III DEVOTIONS FOR COMMUNION :
Page
1. (i) Before the Receiving of our Lord 123 (ii) Immediately before Receiving of our Lord . . .133 (iii) After the Receiving of our Lord 136
2. Before and After Receiving the Most
Holy Sacrament 146

PART IV
GENERAL DEVOTIONS :
I. The Belief. In thee, God Father, believe . . . . . -153
z. A Hymn to the Blessed Trinity and our
Lady. Father y Son and Holy Ghost 156
3. An Intercession to Jesus. Lord God of might !. 161
4. Two Commendations for Death 162
5. The Day of Doom. They that with out en law do rin „ . . .167
6. An Epigram. Heaven ii won . .169
7. Two Thanksgivings :
(i) To the Blessed Trinity. Al mighty God in Trinity . .170
(ii) To Jesus. Lord Jem Christ . 170

xiii Contents]

8. A Prayer of the Five Joys and Five Sorrows of our Lady . . 173
9. A Song to Mary. Hail be thouy Mary . 177
10. Devotions to theGuardian Angel :
(i) A Prayer to a Guardian Angel 179
(ii) A Prayer to the Good Angel 181
n. Of the Abbey of Saint Spirit . .183
NOTES 205
SHORT LIFE OF RICHARD ROLLS . . .217

CHARACTERISTICS OF ENGLISH DEVOTIONS

WHERE are certain characteristics of medieval English devotion which are easy to trace in this collection. They spring, for the most part, from an intense and passionate love for the Sacred Humanity of Jesus Christ. Mother Julian's experience, and her response to it, are an illustration of this tendency. " Then had I a proffer in my reason, as if it had been friendly said to me : Look up to Heaven to His Father ... I answered inwardly with all the might of my soul, and said : Nay ; may not : for Thou art my Heaven ... I would liever have been in that pain till Doomsday than to come to Heaven otherwise than by Him. . . . Thus was I learned to choose Jesus to my Heaven." It any justification for this attitude is needed, we may point to our Lord's own express words :

" No man cometh unto the Father but by me."

It is remarkable how largely this love of the Sacred Humanity has disappeared from non-Catholic English devotion during the last three hundred years : and the fact can only be attributed to the prevalence of Socinian principles. But, however this may be, these old fervent adjurations would be thought by many English people to-day to be uncharacteristic of what they would call the " sober and restrained English spirit." That it has survived, nevertheless, in some quarters is evident by the marked popularity of such hymns as " Jesu, Lover of my soul," and " Rock of Ages cleft for me," both of which, in spirit and phrasing alike, might be medieval poems in a modern dress. It will be remembered, too, that Mr. Shorthouse, in " John Inglesant "—the book in which he treats so acutely of characteristics of English religious thought—represents the religion of his hero as chiefly consisting in this same devotion. " Inglesant's Christianity," he writes, " concentrated itself altogether on what may be called the Idea of Christ ; that is, a lively conception of and attraction to the person of the Saviour. This idea . . . would, no doubt, be inefficient and transitory, were it not for the unique

and mysterious power of attraction which it undoubtedly possesses." The highest moments of Inglesant's spiritual life are so illustrated, culminating in the vision in the hut. "The halo round His head lighted all the hovel, so that the seamless coat He wore, and the marks upon His hands and feet were plainly seen, and the pale alluring face was turned not so much upon the bed and upon the monk as upon Inglesant himself, and the unspeakable glance of the Divine eyes met his." This conception of Mr. Short-house's is the more interesting, as the period of which he writes forms a link about half-way in time between Richard Rolle's day and our own.

As a matter of literal history, too, this intense love of Jesus, so deep in the better and unspoilt English nature, is illustrated by devotional works of the time of the Restoration. For example, what could be more passionate than the following exclamations of love in the writings of Anthony Horneck, chaplain to Charles II. ?

"O my Jesus ! I am not worthy to love thee ! Yet because thou biddest me love thee, and hast told me that my Soul was created on purpose to love thee, I cheerfully resign my Love and Affection to thee ! I desire to love thee ! I wish for nothing more than that I may p«s$ion-xv ii b

Characteristics of English Devotions]

atcly love thee. Whom have I in Heaven to love but thee ? And there is none on Earth that I desire to love more than thyself. For thou art altogether lovely, and thy Love surpasses all the Love of Friends, and the dearest Relations I have.

" O my blessed Redeemer ! I desire to love thee with all my Heart, and with all my Strength: Thou gavest me this Heart and this Strength : And on whom can I bestow it better, than on thee, the Author of it ? Oh, that all that is within me might be turned into Desires, and Inclinations, and Sighs, and Languishings, and Breathings after thee !"

[" The Crucified Jesus."]

Or what could be more tender than Dr. Sutton's " Colloquie of the Soul with Christ touching the Passion " ?

" Lord, wherefore diddest thou suffer thyselj to be sold ?

That I might deliver thee from servitude... Wherefore diddest thou sweat blood f To wash away the spots of thy sin . . . Why wouldest thou be bound ? To loose the bands of thy sins. Why wert thou denied of Peter ? To confess thee before my Father . . .

xvm
[Characteristics of English Devotions
Why wouldest thm be accused ?
To absolve thee.
Why wouldest thou be spitted on ?
To wipe away thy foulness.
Why wouldest thou be whipped ?
That thou mightest be freed from stripes.
Why wouldest thou be lifted up upon the
Cross ? That thou mightest be lifted up to
heaven . ..

Why were thine arms stretched out ? To imbrace thee, O fainting Soul. Why was thy side opened ? To receive thee in. Why didst thou die amidst two thieves ? That thou mightest live in the midst of angels.

Or again yet earlier, at the beginning of the seventeenth century, in Lewes Baily's " Practice of Piety " :

"But I from my soul, humbly with Emmauites intreat thee, O sweet Jesus, to abide with me because it draweth toward night. For the night of temptation, the night of tribulation, yea, my last long night of death approacheth. O blessed Saviour, stay with me therefore now and ever,
xix

Characteristics of English Devotions]

And if thy presence go not home with me, carry me not from hence. Go with me, and live with me, and let neither death nor life separate me from thee. Drive me from myself, draw me unto thee. Let me be sick, but sound in thee ; and in my wealcnesse let thy strength appear. . . . Set me as a seal upon thine heart, and let thy seal be settled upon mine; that I may be out of love with all, that I may be onely in love with thee."

Such quotations, occurring, as some of them do, in books containing much sharp

Protestant controversy, shew how deep such a devotion must have lain and burned in the English heart not to have been extinguished when so much else perished. (It is unnecessary, of course, to adduce quotations from Catholic writers: the unalterable Faith retains its unalterable characteristics.)

From this main principle branch out minor distinctive marks of English piety.

(a). An intimate familiarity with the Saviour.

Here, indeed, it is no wonder that in our days many sincere persons are uneasy; for such an attitude is now so widely accompanied by an in adequate or heretical view of His Person. But where, as in the case of our Catholic forefathers, the grasp upon His Divinity is sure and unfaltering, there is no danger that an intimate affection for His Humanity will lead souls astray, or cause them to treat Him with any lack of reverence. On these heights so near heaven none can tread safely but those who have clear and strong per-ceptionsof dogmatic truth—of that rock that alone can give stability to the pinnacles and spires of prayer. And therefore Richard Rolle can call his Lord his « Dear " and his "Darling," and his " Child the best," without danger of undue familiarity, just because he has such a profound sense of Him as his Maker and his God.

This English familiarity with the Saviour is especially illustrated by the history of the Feast of the Holy Name ; for the loving use of a per sonal name is the sign of personal intimacy. This was an authorised Festival in England by the middle of the fifteenth century, under the title of " The Most Sweet Name Jesu," and was sanctioned and indulgenced by Pope Alex ander VI. at the beginning of the sixteenth century, although it was not accepted into the Roman Calendar until the eighteenth century. Without doubt, then, this was a widely popular devotion in England—(and this is evidenced by Rolle's writings t-ven in this small selection)-long before it had gained any hold elsewhere.

(b) A great reverence and love for the Blessed Virgin Mary.

This, it need hardly be said, is not character istic of modern Protestant devotion. Yet to the old Catholic mystics, vtho recognised that she was and is, in literal fact, the " Mother of God," she was their Mother too, because they were in God and He in them. But devotional writers who in sist so strongly upon the condescending humility of her Divine Son are always at pains to emphasise her own unique exaltation. To them she appears as a " Mother bright " indeed ; as a " Mother of Mercy"; as a " Mother of all wretched and woeful souls" ; but as a great and venerable Queen as well. That there was a measure, too, of familiarity, we see in Mother Julian's vision of her as " a simple maid and a meek, young of age and little waxen above a child, in the stature that she was when she con ceived " ; but, as a rule, " above her is no thing that is made but the blessed manhood of Christ" ; she is the u well and wit of all wis dom " ; the " comely queen " ; the " fairest that ever God found " ; " of all women the fruit and flower"; the "tabernacle of the Trinity."

(c) A deep l&l>e for the details of the Passion.

In almost every mystic the details of the sufferings of our Lord form the ground from which acts of love and contrition and " ruth " spring. This devotion distinguishes sharply the true mystic from his modern imitator, who mis takes vagueness for spirituality, and idealism for intuition. It is supposed to be a mark of modern delicacy and spiritual instinct to despise and shrink from realism ; to dwell upon the Risen Christ, the robed and crowned King, or upon the stainless Child of Bethlehem, and to avoid the vision of the blood-stained Man of Sorrows with His torn limbs. But the true mystic reads the awfulness of sin in the awfulness of the Cross— the story of his own life written so carefully and accurately in blood over the white body and soul of his Saviour—and he sees the infinite love ot God in the infinite sufferings that He so willingly undertook ; the full fragrance of the Beloved is not perceptible except when He is bruised and torn. And therefore the medieval souls of prayer loved to follow Him with tears and " still

mourning" and "love-longing," step by step along the Way of Sorrows ; to finger gently each running wound ; to plunge their whole hands into His side, and there to " feel Christ's Heart so hot loving " them.

[An Introduction to Prayer

Introduction to Draper

thou orderest thyself to pray or to have any devotion, begin by having a privy place away from all manner of noise, and a time of rest without any interruption. Sit there or kneel there, as is most to thine ease.

Then, be thou lord or lady, think well that thou hast a God that made thee of nought, which hath given to thee thy right senses, thy right limbs, and other worldly ease ; more than to some others, as thou mayst see on any day, that live in great dis-ease and much bodily mischief.

Think also how sinful thou art ; and, were it not for the keeping of that good God, thou shouldst fall into all manner of sin by thine own wretchedness; and then thou mayst think sooth ly as of thyself, that there is none so sinful as thou art. Also if thou have any virtue or grace of good living, think it cometh of God's sending, and nothing of thyself. Think also how long and how often God hath suffered thee in sin ;

he would not take thee into damnation when thou hadst deserved it ; but in his goodness hath borne with thee till thou wouldst leave sin and turn to goodness : for he were loth to forsake what he bought so dear with bitter pains.

Also thou mayst think, for that he would not lose thee, he became man, and was born of a maid ; in poverty and tribulation all his life he lived ; and after, for thy love, he would suffer death to save thee by his mercy.

In such manner thou mayst think of his great benefits ; and for the more grace to get to thee compunction, behold with thy ghostly eye his piteous passion.

[Follows a meditation on the passion]

When there cometh devotion, then is time that thou speak for thine own need and for all other quick and dead that trust to thy prayer. Cast down thy body to the ground, and lift up thine heart on high with sorrowful cheer; then make thy moan.

[Follows a prayer on the passion^ containing acts of contrition^ petition and intercession]

In such manner thou mayst pray in the begin ning, and when thou art well entered into devotion thou shalt, peradventure, have better feeling in

prayers and in holy meditations otherwise than I can say or shew.

Good brother or sister, pray then for me which by the teaching of almighty God have written to thee these few words for the helping of thy soul.

PART I THE LOVE OF JESUS

[The Love of Jesus

JESU, who might thy sweetness see And have thereof a clear knowing, All earthly love should bitter be To such, but thine, without leasing. I pray thee, Lord, that lore learn me After thy love to have longing, And firmly set my heart on thee In love of thee to have liking.

So sweet a love on earth none is For one who loves him heartily ; To love him well were greatest bliss For called king of love is he. With this true love I would, I wis, So firmly to him bounden be, That all my heart were wholly his, And other loving liked not me.

The Love of Jesus]
If I by nature love my kin,
(I ever think thus in my thought),
By ties of kin I should begin
At him that made me first of nought.
My soul he set his likeness in,
And all this world for me he wrought
As father true my love to win
My heritage in heaven he bought.

A mother he to me has been, That ere my birth to me took heed ; With baptism washed the nature clean All sin-defiled with Adam's deed. With noble meat he fed my kind For with his flesh he would me feed ; A better food may no man find 5 To lasting life it will us lead.

Brother and sister he is because Himself declared and taught that lore That whoso did his Father's laws Sisters and brothers to him they were ; My nature too he took there-till; Full verily I trust therefore That he will never let me spill, But with his mercy salve my sore. 8

[The Love of Jesus
After his love then I must long For he has mine full dearly bought; When I was gone from him with wrong, For me from heaven to earth he sought ; My wretched nature took, for me, And all his noblesse set at nought, Poverty suffered and penance strong, Ere he to bliss again me brought.

When I was thrall, to make me free My love from heaven to earth him led, For my love only have would he, (And that my soul should saved be) Therefore his life he hazarded : Against my foe he fought for me, Wounded he was, and bitter bled ; His precious blood, full and plenty, Full piteously for me was shed.

His sides all bruised and bloody were That sometime used full bright to be ; His heart was pierced with a spear, His bloody wounds were ruth to see. He paid, I wis, my ransom there, And gave his life for guilt of me ; His doleful death should grieve me dear. And pierce my heart for pure pity. 1

The Love of jesus
For pity my heart should break in two If to his kindness I took heed ; Reason I was of all his woe ; He suffered hard for my misdeed. To lasting life that I should go His death he bore in his man-head ; And, when he willed, to live also He rose again through his Godhead.

To heaven he went with highest bliss When he had vanquished his battail. His banner broad displayed is, When so my foe will me assail. Well ought mine heart then to be hh. For he is friend that ne'er will fail ; And nothing he desires, I wis, Save my true love for his travail.

Thus for my sake my spouse would fight, And wounded was for me full sore ; For love of me his death was dight : What kindness might he do me more ? To love like him I never might, But love him lcally I should therefore, And work his will with works aright, As he taught me with lovely lore. 10

[The Love of Jesus
His lovely lore with works fulfill Well should I strive, if I were kind, By night and day to

work his will, And have him evermore in mind. But ghostly enemies grieve me ill, And fleshly frailty makes me blind ; Therefore his mercy I take me till, For better help I can none find.

No better help is there to me Than to his mercy me to take; Who with his blood has made me free, And me, a wretch, his son would make. I pray that Lord for his pity For sin me never to forsake, But give me grace sin for to flee, That in his love I never slake.

Ah ! JesUy for the love in thee
Remember me when I shall wend :
With stedfast truth establish me
And guard me safely from the fiend.
For mercy pardon all amiss
From wicked works my soul defend
And bring me y Lord into thy bliss
With thee to dwell without en end. Amen,
The Love of Jesus]
llufjarfc &e (Eastre's iayrr to
Oratio magistri Ricardi de Castre^ quam ipse posuit,
JESU, Lord that madest me And with thy blesse'd blood has bought, Forgive that I have grieved thee
With word, with will and eke with thought.
Jesu, in whom is all my trust,
That died upon the high rood-tree, Withdraw my heart from fleshly lust,
And from all worldly vanity.
Jesu, for thy sore wounds' smart
Thy feet and hands that pierced through,
Make me meek and low of heart, And thee to love as I should do.
Jesu, for thy bitter wound
That pierced through to thy heart's root, For sin that so my heart hath bound
Grant that thy blood may be my boot ! Help 12
\'7bThe Love of Jesus
And, Jesu Christ, to thee I call
That art my God, and full of might,
Keep thou me clean lest that I fall In deadly sin by day or night.
Jesu, grant thou me mine asking, Perfect patience in my dis-ease ;
And never may I do that thing
That should thee any-wise displease.
Jesu, that art our heavenly king,
Soothfast man and God also, Give me grace of good ending,
And them that I am 'holden to.
Jesu, for the deadly tears
That thou once sheddedst for my guilt, Hearken to me and speed my prayers,
And spare me that I be not spilt.
Jesu, for them I thee beseech That anger thee in any wise ;
Withhold from them thy hand of wreak, And let them live in thy service.
Jesu, most comfort for to see
For thy dear saints both all and one,
Comfort them that care-full be,

And help them that be woe-begone. 13

The Love of Jesus

Jesu, keep thou them that be good, Amend them that have grieved thee,
And send them fruits of earthly food As each man needeth in his degree.
Jesu, that art the ghostly stone Of holy church in all the earth,
Bring thy folds and flocks in one,
And rule them rightly with one shepherd.
Jesu, for all thy blessed blood,
Bring, if thou wilt, those souls to bliss From whom I have had any good,
And spare what they have done amiss.

[The Love of Jesus

Firtues of tfte name

Introduction.

IF thou wilt to be with God, and to have grace to rule thy life, and to come to the joy of love; this name Jesu —fasten it so fast in thine heart, that it come never out of thy thought. And when thou speakest to him, and sayest Jesu^ through custom, it shall be in thine ear joy, and in thy mouth honey, and in thine heart melody. For thou shalt think joy to hear the name of Jesu named, sweetness to speak it, mirth and song to think on it. If thou think on Jesu Continually and hold it stably, it purgeth thy sin, it kindleth thy heart, it clarifieth thy soul, it removeth anger, it doeth away slowness, it bringeth in love fulfilled of charity, it chaseth the devil, it putteth out dread, it openeth heaven, it maketh contemplative men. Have Jesu often in mind; For all vices and phantoms it putteth from the lover or it. Also thereto hail Mary often, both day and night, '5

The Love of Jesus]

and then much joy and love shalt thou feel. If thou do after this sort, thou needest not greatly covet many books. Hold love in heart and in work, and thou hast all that we may say or write; for fulness of law is charity; in that hangeth all.

The Meditation.

OLEUM effusum nomen tuum. That is in English, Ointment outpoured is thy name.

This name is ointment outpoured, for Jesu, the Word of God, has taken man's nature. Jesu, thou fulfillest in work what thou art called in name:—(in truth he saves man,—he whom we call Saviour,)—therefore Jesu is thy name.

Ah! ah! that wonderful name! Ah! that delightable name! This is the name that is above all names, the highest name of all, without which no man hopes for health. This name is in mine ear heavenly sound, in my mouth honeyful sweetness.

Soothly, Jesu, desirable is thy name, lovable and comfortable. None so sweet joy may be conceived, none so sweet song may be heard, none so sweet and delightable solace may toe had in mind.

Soothly, nothing so slackens fell flames; 16

[The Love of Jesus

destroys ill thoughts; puts out venomous affections; does away curious and vain occupations from us.

This name Jesu y leally holden in mind, draws out vices by the root; plants virtues; sows charity; pours in savour of heavenly things; wastes discord; forms again peace; gives lasting rest; does away grievousness of fleshly desires; turns all earthly things to nought; fills the loving with ghostly joy.

Wherefore what can fail him that covets ever lastingly to love the name of Jesu? Soothly he loves and he yearns for to love ; for we have known that the love of God stands in such manner that the more we love the more we long to love. Wherefore it is said, Qui edunt me adhuc esurient, et qui bibunt me adhuc sitiunt; that is to say, They that eat me hunger yet, and they that drink me thirst yet.

Therefore itself delightable and covetable is the name of Jesu and the love of it. Therefore joy shall not fail him that covets busily for to love him whom angels yearn for to behold. Angels ever see and ever they yearn for to see ; and they are so filled that their filling does not away their desire, and so their desire does not away their filling.

The Love of Jesus]

Therefore, Jesu, all shall joy that love thy name. Soothly shall they joy now by the in-pouring of grace, and in time to come by the sight of joy ; and therefore shall they joy, for that they love thy name. In sooth, were they not loved, they might not joy; and they that love more shall joy more ; for why ?—joy comes of love.

Therefore he that loves not, he shall evermore be without joy.

Therefore many poor wretches of the world, trowing that they shall joy with Christ, shall sorrow without end ; and why ? For that they loved not the name of Jesu. Whatsoever ye do, if ye give all that ye have unto the needy, except ye love the name of Jesu ye travail in vain. They alone may joy in Jesu that love him in this life; and they that fill them with vices and venomous delights, doubtless they shall be put out of joy.

Also know all that the name of Jesu is healthful, fruitful, and glorious. Therefore who shall have health that loves it not ? Or who shall bear the fruit before Christ, that has not the flower ? And joy shall he not see that in his joying loved not the name of Jesu. The wicked shall be done away, that he see not the joy of God.

[The Love of Jesus

Soothly the righteous seek the joy and the life, and they find it in Jesu whom they love.

I went about those covetous of riches, and I found not Jesu.

I ran by the fleshly wantons, and I found not Jesu.

I sat in companies of worldly mirth, and I found not Jesu.

In all these I sought Jesu, but I found him not ; for he let me wit by his grace that he is not found in the land of soft living.

Therefore I turned by another way, and I ran about by poverty ; and I found Jesu, pure-born in the world, laid in a crib and lapped in clothes.

I went by suffering of weariness, and I found Jesu weary in the way, tormented with hunger, thirsty and cold, filled with reproofs and blames.

I sat by myself, fleeing the vanities of the world, and I found Jesu fasting in the desert, praying alone in the mount.

I ran by the pain of penance, and I found Jesu bounden, scourged, given gall to drink, nailed to the cross, hanging on the cross, and dying on the cross.

Therefore Jesu is not found in riches, but in poverty : not in delights, but in penance : not in

The Love of Jesus]

wanton joying, but in bitter weeping : not among many, but in loneliness.

Soothly an evil man finds not Jesu, for where he is he seeks him not. He endeavours to seek Jesu in the joy of the world, where never shall he be found.

Soothly therefore the name of Jesu is healthful, and need behoves that it be loved of all that covet salvation. He covets well his salvation that keeps busily in him the name of Jesu.

Soothly I have no wonder if the tempted fall, who put not in lasting mind the name of Jesu.

Safely may he (or such as he) choose to live alone, that has chosen the name of Jesu to his own possession; for there may no wicked spirit do harm, where Jesu is much in mind or named in mouth.

[The Love of Jesus

Hobf Of

OVE is life that lasteth aye, Here it is in Christ made fast, Weal nor woe it loosen may,

As have written men wisest. The night it turneth into day, Travail it turneth into rest ; If thou wilt do as I thee say,

Thou shalt then be with the best.

Love is light, and a burden fine,

Love gladdeneth both young and old ; Love is withouten any pine,

As lovers have me told. Love is ghostly, delicious as wine,

That maketh men both big and bold ; To that love I shall so fast tyne, Hold.

That I in heart it ever hold. 21

The Love of Jesus]

But all fleshly love shall fare,

As QO the flowers of May j And shall be lasting never more

But as it were an hour of day ; And sorrowing after that full sore

Their lust, their pride and all their play, They that love thus are cast in care

And into pain that lasteth aye.

Jem ! God's own Son thou art.

Lord of most high majesty, Send verily love into my hearty

Only to covet thee ! Despoil my liking of this world^

My love that thou may be; Take thou my heart into thy ward.

And set me in stability.

Jesu ! thou the maiden's son

Me with thy blood hast dearly bought ; Pierce my soul with thy spear anon,

That much love in men hath wrought. I long that thou lead me to thy sight,

And fasten there in thee my thought; In thy sweetness make my heart light,

That all my woe may wax to nought 22

[Tie Love of Jesus

My love is ever in sore sighing,

While I linger in this way. My love is after thee longing.

And bindeth me both night and day : Till I come unto my king,

That there I dwell beside him may, And see myself his fair shining,

In life that lasteth aye.

I sit and sing of love-longing

That now within my breast is bred. Jesu ! my king and my joying !

Why am I not before thee led ? Full well I wot in my yearning

In highest joy I shall be fed. Jesu ! bring me to thy dwelling,

For the blood that thou hast bled !

Doomed he was on a cross to hang,

He that was fair angels' food ; On him their scourges sore they swang,
When that he all bounden stood. His breast was blackened with beating,
Not spilled was his blood ; They thorn-crowned that heavenly king
That done was on the rood.

The Love of Jesus]

White was his naked breast,
And red his bloody side ; Wan was his face fairest,
His wounds were deep and wide : The Jews then would not rest
From paining him that tide ; All he suffered that was wisest
His blood to let down-glide.

Death and life began to strive,
Whether might be master there ; Life was slam and rose again :
(Ma) .we fare into bliss full fair !) Let him that bought thee have thy thought,
And let him lead it to his lore ! To Christ full gladly give thy heart,—
And so to love him evermore.

I sigh, I sob both day and night
For one that is so fair of hue ; There nothing is my heart may light,
Saving his love that is so true. For whoso had him in his sight,
Or in his heart him knew, His grief should turn to gladness bright,
His longing into glee. 24

[The Love of Jesus

In mirth he liveth night and day
That loveth that sweet child. Anger will from him away
Were he ne'er so wild. Jesu it is, forsooth to say,
Of all mankind most meek and mild ; Him that in heart loveth him that day
He will from evil shield.

For very love my heart will burst
When I that fair beloved behold ; Love is full fair where it is fast
That never will be cold. Love robbeth us of nightly rest ;
In grace it makes us wondrous bold, Of all men's works, love is the best
As holy men to me have told.

There's none alive on earth may tell
Of this love all the great sweetness, He that in love can stedfast dwell,
His joy is evermore endless. Ah ! God forbid he should to hell,
That of love-longing cannot cease ! Or that his foes him ever quell,
Or that he his love should lose ! 25

The Love of Jesus]

Jesu is love that lasteth aye,
To him alone is our longing. Jesu the night turneth to day,
And darkness black into day-spring, Jesu ! think on us now and aye
For thee alone we hold our king ! Jesu ! give grace that so we may
Love thee ever without ending. Amen.

[The Love of Jesus

to

JESU CHRIST, saint Mary's son, Through whom the world was meetly wrought ;

I pray thee come and dwell in me, And of all filths cleanse thou my thought.

Jesu Christ, my God very, That of our Lady dear was born ; Help me for ever and for aye And let me ne'er for sin be 'lorn.

Jesu Christ, God's Son of heaven, That died for me upon the rood ; I pray thee hear my simple staven Through virtue of thy holy blood.

Jesu Christ, that on third day From death to life rose through thy might ; Give thou me grace thy due to pay, And thee to worship day and night. 27

The Love of Jesus]

Jesu, of whom all goodness springs, Whom all men ought to love by right; Make me give heed to thy biddings, And them fulfill with all my might.

Jesu Christ, that bare for me Pains and angers bitter and fell ; Let me ne'er be parted from thee Nor bear the bitter pains of hell.

Jesu Christ, well of mercy, Of pity and of all goodness ; For all the sins that ever did I I pray thee give me forgiveness.

Jesu, to thee I make my moan, Jesu, to thee I call and cry ; Let never my soul with sin be slain, For the greatness of thy mercy.

Jesu, that is my dear Saviour, Be thou my joy and my solace, My help, my health, my comforter, And my succour in every place.

Jesu, that with thy blood me bought, Jesu, make me clean of sin ; 28

[The Love of Jesus

And with thy love wound thou my thought, And let me never from thee twin.* » p ar t.

Jesu, I covet to love thee, And that is wholly my yearning ; Therefore to love thee learn thou me, And I thy love shall sing.

Jesu, thy love into me send And with thy love do thou me feed ; Jesu, thy love aye to me lend, Thy love be ever my soul's meed.

Jesu, set thou my heart alight ; May thy love make me aye forsake All worldly joy, both day and night; And joy in thee alone to make.

Jesu, in me thy love inspire,
That nothing but thee may I seek ;
In thy love set my soul afire ;
May thy love make me mild and meek.
Jesu, my joy and my loving
Jesu, my comfort clear ! Jesu, my God ! Jesu, my king !
Jesu, withouten peer ! 2Q

The Love of Jesus]
Jesu, my dear and my one joy !
Delight thou art to sing ! Jesu, my mirth and my melody 1
Into thy love me bring.
Jesu, Jesu, my honey sweet,
My heart, my comforting ! Jesu, my woes do thou down beat,
And to thy bliss me bring.
Jesu, with thy love wound my thought,
And lift my heart to thee ; Jesu, my soul that thou dear bought
Thy lover make to be.
Now, Jesu, Lord, give thou me grace,
If so it be thy will, That I may come into thy place

And dwell aye with thee still. Amen,

[The Love of Jesus

Comfort of

JESUS, that sprang of Jesse's root (As preached to us the old prophet \] Full soft and sweet, both flower and fruit To soul of man a savour sweet ; Jesu, to man thou broughtest boot, When Gabriel first did Mary greet, To fell our foemen under foot In her thou set thy seemly seat : A maiden was thy mother meet Of whom thou tookest flesh for us ; — That ye both may my woes down-beat So be my comfort, Christ Jesus.

 Jesu, thou art all wisdom's wit,
 Of God thy Father full of might ;
 For soul of man, to ransom it,
 In poor apparel thou wert pight.
 Jesu, thou wert in cradle knit,
 And wrapped in garments day and night ;
 The Love of Jesus]

In Bethlehem born, (as gospel writ,) With angels' song and heaven's light : A bairn, and born of maiden bright, Thy comely kiss was full courteous ;— Through virtue of that most sweet sight, So be my comfort, Christ Jesus.

 Jesu, that wert in years full young, Fair and fresh in face and hue, When as thou wert in thralldom flung, Tormented sore by many a Jew, When blood and water were out-wrung, Thy body beaten black and blue ; As clot of clay thou wert forth-flung, And dead in tomb then men thee threw, But great grace from thy grave up-grew : Thou rose alive to comfort us.— For her love that this counsel knew, So be my comfort, Christ Jesus.

 Jesu, thou very God and man, Two natures knit in one person ; The wondrous work that thou began Thou hast fulfilled in flesh and bone : Out of this world didst quickly win, Uprising of thyself alone. 3*

 [The Love of Jesus

For mightily thou rose and ran Straight to thy Father on the throne. Now dareth man make no more moan ; For sake of man thou wroughtest thus, And God with man is made at one :— So be my comfort, Christ Jesus.

 Christ Jesu, holy Lord and kind,
 That maid was blessed, that brought forth thee,
 At last for her when thou did'st send
 In bliss of heaven with thee to be ;
 From out this world when she did wend,
 Her body and soul, on high to see,
 Were set above all angels' kind,
 Enthroned before the Trinity.
 There may the son his mother see
 In heaven on high to succour us :—
 Thou peerless princess pray for me,
 And be my comfort, Christ Jesus.

 Jesu, my sovereign Saviour, Almighty God who rulestall, Christ, do thou be my governour; From faith in thee let me not fall, Jesu ! my joy and my succour ! In my body and soul also God, do thou be the strengthening power ; 33 c

 The Love of Jesus]

And give me guidance in my woe. O Lord, thou makest friend of foe ; Let me not live in languor thus, But see and stay my deep sorrow,— And be my comfort, Christ Jesus.

Jesu, to thee I cry and plead ;
Great prince of peace, to thee I pray ;
Thou wouldest bleed for mankind's need,
And suffer many a fearful fray.
In all my dread do thou me feed
With perfect patience now and aye 5
My life to lead in word and deed
As best I may thy love repay,
And to die well when comes my day—
Jesu ! that died on tree for us,
Let me not be the devil's prey,
But be my comfort, Christ Jesus. Amen.

[The Love of Jesus

Sfiou Sbongs to

JESU, as thou me made and bought, Be thou my love and all my thought And help that I be to thee brought ; Withouten thee may I do nought !

II. A Rhythm

JESU CHRIST, God's Son of heaven, King of kings and Lord of lords,
My Lord and my God : For the meekness of thy clean incarnatio'). And through the merit of thy hard passion,

Save us from damnation,
Succour us in temptation,
And give us thy benison,
And of all our wickedness full pardon.
And full remission,
The Love of Jesus]
Through true contrition,
Naked confession,
And worthy satisfaction. Grant us alway, Lord God,
In heaven an aye-lasting mansion,
And ever to see the cheer-full vision Of thy fair face. For the love that thou shewest to mankind,
Amen.

III

JESU, at thy will I pray that I may be ; All my heart fulfill With perfect love to thee: That I have done ill, Jesu, forgive thou me ; And let me never spill, Jesu, for thy pity. Amen.

IV

JESU, since thou canst do thy will, And nothing is that thee can let ; With thy grace my heart fulfill, My love and liking in thee set.

[The Love of Jesus

JESU CHRIST, have mercy on me, As thou art king of majesty ;
And forgive me my sins all
That I have done, both great and small ;
And bring me, if it be thy will

To heaven to dwell aye with thee still Amen.

VI

TN world of worlds without ending Jesu be thanked, my heavenly king ! All my heart I give to thee, Great right it is that so it be : With all my will I worship thee. Jesu, blessed mayst thou be ! I from my heart give thanks to thee, For good that thou hast done to me. Sweetest Jesu, grant me this That I may come unto thy bliss; That with angels for to sing This sweet song of thy loving Sanctus, Sanctus, Sanctus— Jesu, grant that it be thus. Amen. 37

The Love of Jesus]

vii

JESU mine, grant me thy grace, And for amendment might and space, To keep thy word and do thy will, To choose the good and leave the ill, And that it so may be Good Jesu, grant it me. Amen,

(The Love o/ Jesus

, to ;

OMOST sweetest spouse of my soul, Christ Jesu;

Desiring heartily evermore for to be with thee, in mind and will, and to let no earthly thing be so nigh mine heart as thee, Christ Jesu ; —

And that I dread not for to die, for to go to thee, Christ Jesu ; —

And that I may evermore say to thee with glad cheer, My Lord, my God, my sovereign Saviour, Christ Jesu ; —

I beseech thee heartily to take me, a sinner, unto thy great mercy and grace. For I love thee with all mine heart, with all my mind, and with all my might ; and nothing so much in earth, nor above the earth as I do thee, my sweet Lord, Christ Jesu.

And, for that I have not loved thee nor wor shipped thee above all things, as my Lord, my God, and my Saviour, Christ Jesu ; — 39

The Love of Jesus]

I beseech thee, with meekness and contrite heart, for mercy and for forgiveness of my great unkindness, for the great love that thou shewedst for me and all mankind, what time thou ofFeredst thy glorious body, God and man, unto the cross, there to be crucified and wounded ; and unto thy glorious heart a sharp spear, whence ran out plenteously blood and water for the redemption and salvation of me and all mankind.

And thus having remembrance stedfastly in my heart, Christ Jesu ;—

I doubt not but that thou wilt be full nigh me, and comfort me both bodily and ghostly with thy glorious presence; And at the last bring me unto thine everlasting bliss, the which shall never have end. Amen.

[The Love of Jesus

Draper for (State anK

|j MOST dear Lord and Saviour ; sweet Jesu, I beseech thy most courteous goodness and benign favour to be to me, most wretched crea ture, my favourable Lord, keeper and defender ; and in all necessities and needs to be my shield and protection against all mine enemies bodily and ghostly.

Merciful Jesu, I have none other trust, hope, nor succour, but in thee alonely, rny dear Lord : sweet Jesu ; the which of thine infinite goodness made me of nought, like unto thy most excellent image. And when I was lost by my first fathei Adam's sin, with thy precious blood, dear Lord, thou redeemedst me, and since then, ever daily, most graciously, with thy gifts of grace most lovingly thou feedest me.

Grant me therefore, most gracious Lord and Saviour, to dread thee and love thee above all things in this present life, and after in joy and bliss without end.

Sweet Jesu. Amen.

PART II THE PASSION OF JESUS

[Tie Passion o

THE passion of Jesu Christ confounds the fiend : it destroys his deceits and his snares : it slackens fleshly temptations : it clarifies the mind to covet only Jesu Christ's love. Fasten in thine heart the memory of his passion : I wot nothing, that shall so inwardly take thine heart to covet God's love, and to desire the joy of heaven, and to despise vanities of this world, as stedfast thinking on the hurts and the wounds, and on the death of Jesu Christ. It will raise thy thought above earthly pleasure, and set thine heart burning in Christ's love, and purchase into thy soul delightability and savour of heav(

The Passion of Jesus]

CWEET Lord Jesu Christ, I thank thee and yield thee grace for that sweet prayer and for that holy orison that thou madest before the holy passion for us on the mount of Olivet.

Adoramus te Christ e et benedicimus tibi quia per crucem tuam redemisti mundum. Pater noster. Ave Maria.

Sweet Lord Jesu Christ, I thank thee and yield thee grace for that great fearfulness that thou hadst for our sakes, when thou became so full of anguish that an angel of heaven came to comfort thee, when thou sweatedst blood for anguish.

I pray thee, Lord, and beseech thee, for thy sweet mercy, that thou be mine help in all mine anguish and my temptations, and send me, Lord, the angel of counsel and of comfort in all my needs, that I may turn, through that sweat, out

[The Passion of Jesus

of all sickness of soul and body into life and health.

Adoramus &c. Pater. Ave.

Sweet Jesu, I thank thee and yield thee grace for the pains and anguishes and shames and felonies that men did thee, and that by treachery; men binding thee as a thief, without mercy or pity. Lord, I thank thee for those sweet and piteous paces that thou wentest for love of us toward thine own pain and thine own death.

I pray thee, Lord and beseech thee that thou unbind us of the bonds of all our sins, as thou suffered to be bound for love of us.

Adoramus. Pater. Ave. I thank thee, sweet Lord Jesu Christ, for the pains and for the shames that thou suffered before the high priests and the masters of the Law, and thine enemies; for buffets and for nakedness, and for many other shames that thou suffered, And, among other, I thank thee, Lord, for that look that thou looked to thy disciple that had forsaken thee, saint Peter ; thou looked to him with a glance of mercy when thou wert in thy most anguish and thy most pain : openly thou shewed there the love and the charity that thou had to us, that neither shame nor pain nor any-47

The Passion of Jesus]

thing else may withdraw thine heart from us, so far as in thee is. Sweet Lord, full of mercy and pity, may we through that blessed look of thine, turn to thy grace and repent us of our trespass and of our misdeed, so that with saint Peter we may come to thy mercy.

Adoramus. Pater. Ave.

I thank thee, sweet Lord Jesu Christ, for all the pains and torments and scornings and slanderings and shames that men did and said to thee that night in that hard prison that they held thee in.

Lord, I pray and beseech that thou give me patience and strength for to withstand stedfastly against all the assailings and temptations of my foes and of mine enemies ghostly and bodily.

Adoramus. Pater. Ave.

Lord Jesu Christ, I thank thee for all the pains and shames that thou suffered before Pilate, and for all thy paces and thy steps that thou wentest for me in all that sorrow, now hitherward, now thitherward, now before one, and now before another.

I thank ; and I beseech thee, Lord, by all these pains and these shames and these grievances and the paces that thou wentest then in that

[The Passion of Jesus

same time for love of us, that thou guide and direct our goings and our steps to thee-ward, and to thy service.

Adoramus. Pater. Ave.

Sweet Lord Jesu Christ, I thank thee for the pains that thou suffered for us, and for the sweet blood that thou bled for us, when thou wert so sore beaten and bounden to the pillar that the blood is yet seen on the pillar.

I pray thee and beseech thee as my dear Lord that that sweet blood that thou bled so plenti fully for me may be full remission for my soul.

Adoramus. Pater. Ave. Sweet Lord Jesu Christ I thank thee for the pains and shames that thou suffered for us of thy sweet will, when thou wert clad in purple for to shame thee, and with the crown of thorns for to pain thy sweet head, and when they kneeling in scorn called thee Lord, King, and Master : and withal that on thy sweet face spitted so foully, and so foully defiled thy fair face with the foul spittle of the foul cursed Jews, and buffeted and smote and beat on thy sweet head withal : And for thy bitter wounds I thank thee, for thy pains and for thy sweet blood that ran down and streamed from thy blessed face.

The Passion of Jesus]

I pray and beseech thee, dear Lord, that thou defend us from sin, and from the shame that we have deserved for sin.

Adoramus. Pater. Ave.

Sweet Lord Jesu Christ, I thank thee that thou wertsobe-bled then,so crowned with thorns before all the folk, and thy sweet face so spitted on and so smeared with the foul spitting of their cursed mouths. Then wert thou on each side forced and hurried to violent death, and doomed to foul death of hanging—blessed and thanked be thou !

I beseech thee, dear Lord, that of thy great mercy thou give me grace and wisdom for to judge and doom myself, for the salvation of my soul.

Adoramus. Pater. Ave. Sweet Lord Jesu Christ, I thank thee for the pains and the shames that thou suffered so sweetly and so gladly ; now for to drag thee, now for to push thee so shamefully ; now for to smite thee, now for to beat thee so sore and so felly; and for to bear thine own rood on thy sweet naked back—as it were a thief that bare his own gallows for to be hanged on it himself—to the mount of Calvary, where men executed wicked men and thieves, whether they were thieves or murderers 50

[The Passion of Jesus

and there thou suffered them to do thee on the cross.

Dear Lord Jesu, mercy ! thou that art the well of mercy, why will not mine heart burst and cleave in two ? How shall it ever endure, when it run neth in my mind how woe-begone thou wert at thy stripping ! when the false Herod let take thy garment from thee, and it cleaved fast with the blood of that hard scourging to the flesh of thy body that sore was beaten and rawed, and rent thy blessed skin ! the garment cleaved to it, and was dried to it; thy flesh was so tender, so sick and so sore, that they drew it off thy body piteously and painfully. ... Ah ! Lord, I see thy red blood run down thy cheeks, streams after each stroke, before and behind. Thy crown hath all rent the skin of thine head ; each thorn that is there pierceth to thy brain. Alas! that I should live and see my gracious Lord so suffering and so meek ;—that never trespassed, so shamefully bedight ! The moaning and the groaning, the sorrow and the sighing, the pain of his face !— I would it were my death ! The Crown of all bliss, that crowns all the blessed, and is King of all kings, and is Lord of all lords, is by hell hounds crowned with thorns ! The Worship of heaven, despised and defouled ! He that shaped

The Passion of Jesus]

the sun, and all that is aught, he of whose gift is all that is in earth,—he had not where he might hide his head ; but is become so poor, to make us rich, that he goeth all naked, in sight of all the folk.

Ah ! Lord, thy sorrow ! Why were it not my death ?

Now they lead thee forth, naked as a worm, the tormentors about thee, and armed knights. The press of the people was wonderfully strong ; they hurled thee about and harried thee so shamefully ; they spurned thee with their feet, as if thou had been a dog. I see in my soul how ruefully thou goest ; thy body is all bleeding, so rawed and so bloodied ; thy crown is so sharp that presseth on thy head ; thy hair, all stickied with the blood, moveth in the wind ; thy lovely face so wan and so swollen with buffeting and with beating, with spitting, with spouting ; thy blood runs down it, so that I shudder at the sight : so loathely and so horrible have the Jews made thee, that thou art liker to a leper than to a clean man. The cross is so heavy, so high and stark, that they hanged on thy bare back, and trussed there so hard. Ah ! Lord, the groaning that thou made, so sore and so hard did it rest on thy bones ! Thy body is so sick, so feeble and so weary, what with

[The Passion of Jesus

long fasting before thou wert taken, and all night awake without any rest ; with beating, with buffeting so greatly oppressed, that thou goest all stooping, and heavy is thy face : the flesh where the cross resteth is all rawed ; the veins and the arteries are wan and livid ; the pain of that burden oppresseth thee so sore that each foot that thou goest it pierceth to thy heart.

Thus in this groaning and in this greatpain thou goest out of Jerusalem towards thy death. The city is so great, the people so much, that the folk come running out of each street; then stand up the folk, and so great is the reek, that men may wonder that think thereon. With such a procession of worldly wondering, was never thief led to death. Some there were of the common people that sighed sore and wept for thy woe, that knew thee so tormented, and that it was for envy ; for the princes and the high-priests, that, burdened men with the law, did thee to death for thy true sayings, when thou would reprove them of their errors. They knew it was outrage and wrong that thou suffered, and followed thee weeping and sighing sore. Then thou said a thing that afterwards came to pass: thou bade them weep for themselves, and for the great vengeance that should fall for thy death on them

The Passion of Jesus

and on their children, and on all the city that afterwards was destroyed, and for the vengeance of their own guilt that they should be driven out of their place.

Ah ! Lord, the sorrow that fell on thy heart when thou cast thine eyes on thy mother !

Thou saw her follow after among the great press ; as a woman out of herself she wrung her hands, weeping and sighing she cast her arms about, the water of her eyes dropped at her feet; she fell in dead swoon once afterwards for sorrow of the pains that smote to her heart. The sorrow that she made, and her great dolour, increased many-fold all thine other pains. So when she wist that this was so, then was her sorrow worse again, and thou also did weep for her : so was the sorrow of you both, either for other, waxen many-fold with sorrow upon sorrow. The love of your hearts that above all other loves was surpassing burning-keen, made you to burn, either for other, with sorrow unlike to any other woe ; as the love was surpassing, so was the sorrow peerless—it pierced to your hearts, as it were death.

Ah ! Lady, mercy ! Why wert thou so bold as to follow so nigh among so many keen foes ? how was it that womanly cowardice or maidenly 54

[The Passion of Jesus

shame had not withdrawn thee apart ? for it was not seemly for thee to follow such a rout, so vile and so shameful and so terrible to see ! But thou had no care for the dread of any man, nor for aught else that could hinder thee, but, as if out of thyself for dolour and for sorrow of thy son's passion, all thine heart was set firm. The love of you both was so keen, either to other, and so burning-hot; thy sighings were so fervent ; the dolour of your faces was deadly woe ! The love and the sorrow that pierced thy breast, hindered thee from recking aught of bodily dread, and of the world's shame, and of all manner of hind rances, so out of thyself hath thy sorrow made thee.

Ah ! Lady, for that sorrow that thou suffered for thy son's passion—for that should have been mine own, for I had deserved it, and much worse ; I was the cause of it, and I was the guilty one. Since then the dear wounds are mine own right, get me one of them, for thy mercy !— a prick at mine heart of that same pain, a drop of that pity to follow him with. Since all that woe is my right, get me of mine own, and be not thou so wrongful as to withhold it all. Al though thy woe be dear to thee, yet art not thou very rich ? share with this poor soul that hath 55

The Passion of Jesus']

little or none of it. Thou that sighest so sore, give me of thy sighings, that I, who began that woe, may sigh with thee. I ask not, dear Lady, castles nor towers, nor other world's vealth, nor the sun nor the moon nor the bright stars, but wounds of pity is all my desire, pain and com passion of my Lord Jesus Christ. Holding myself worst and unworthiest of all men, I havt appetite for pain, to beseech of my Lord a drop of his red blood to make my soul bloody, a drop of that water to wash it with. Ah ! for that mercy, Lady, that art mother of mercy, succour of all sorrow, and cure of all ill, made the mother of all wretched and woeful souls, hearken to this wretch and visit thy child ! sow in mine heart, that is hard as stone, one spark of compassion for that dear passion, a wound of that pity to supple it with !

Ah ! Lord, that pain that evil Jews, so cruel and so keen, at the mount of Calvary, without mercy pained thee with ! They cast the cross down flat on the ground, and with strong ropes bound thine hands and thy feet, and laid thee thereon ; they drew and strained thee straight, on breadth and length, by hands and by feet ; and they drive in the nails, first in the one hand ; then they draw hard, and after drive in that 5°

[The Passion of Jesus

other. The nails were blunt at the point, that they should burst the skin and the flesh ; they dug open thine hands and thy feet with the blunt nails, for the more pain. Foderunt manus meas et pedes meos.

Glorious Lord, so dolefully dight, so ruefully strained upright on the rood, for thy much meek ness, thy mercy, thy might, do thou mend all my misery by aid of thy blood !

Ah! Lord, the pity that I now see! thy wounds in thy straining reach so wide; thy limbs are so tender! Thou liest, rawed and red, strained on the cross; the sharp crown on thine head that presseth thee so sore; thy face is so swollen that first was so fair; thy sinews and thy bones start out so stark, that thy bones may be numbered; the streams of thy red blood run as the flood; thy wounds are bloodied and fearful to look on; the sorrow that thy mother maketh increaseth thy woe!

Ah! Lord, king of might, that wouldest leave thy might, and become as unmighty, my wrongs to right; why do I speak thus and beat the wind? I speak of the feeling of thee, and I find no taste; I blunder in my working as a man that is blind: I study in my thoughts, and waste all thy works. It is the tokening of my death,

The Passion of Jesus]

and the filth of my sin, that hath slain my soul and choked it therein, andstoppeth all the savour, so that I may not feel thee, I that have so shamefully been thy traitor untrue. It might be a prison, glorious Lord, to thy Godhead—the foulness of my shame, the sorrow of my soul, the filth of my mouth: if I look thereon, it defileth thy name: so may I in no manner taste the sweetness of thee, for I have lost through sin to have liking of such comfort; for I blunder gladly in lusts of many divers sins. But thou, glorious Lord, thou quickenest the dead, and hast converted many-fold, and brought them to heavenly meed: those born blind thou enlightened, as I read in the Book :—(it betokeneth ghostly works, no doubt). Quicken me, Lord Jesu Christ, and give me grace that I may feel some of the savour of ghostly sweetness: lend me of thy light, that I may have somewhat of sight in my soul, to quench my thirst. (But well I wot this that I have read, that whoso yearneth and seeketh aright, though he feel it not, yet hath he the love of thy Godhead, though he wot it not. This saying and others such set before us that if a man find no savour, let him think himself an outcast, rebuking and reviling and seeing his own weakness, and resigning himself as un-

[The Passion of Jesus

worthy to have devotion, or any such special gift of our Lord God, whensoever he may find no devotion. Then shall he soonest get the gift of his grace.)

Then there went after the cross many Jews enough, and raised it up, and lifted it up on high, with all the power that they had, and set it hard into the pit of the hole that was made before; so that thy wounds burst and ran sore out, and thy body hanged all shaken—woe-begone was thee!

Lord, woe was thee then, with the sore wounds of thy feet and of thine hands that were above all men's most tender, and that bare all the weight of thy blessed body that was so fair and so heavy. That sore sorrow thy mother beheld that was so lovely and so meek and so mild: she fell down oftentimes, sighing now and then; the sorrow pierced her breast, as it were death: her head she hanged down dolefully, her hands she wrung, the tears were full abundant that there she wept. The sighings and the sorrows that she made there were an increase of thy woe, and made it many-fold more. The place was so dreadful and full of groans, the foulness of the carcases smote in thy nostrils. Thus pained was thou in thy five senses, to heal therewith our trespass that we with our senses have wrought.

The Passion of Jesus]

Against that we trespassed with our seeing, thou would of the Jews be blindfolded.

Against the sin of our nostrils, the smell of the carcases as thou hanged on the rood smote in thy nostrils, so that it was to thee full grievous.

Against our tasting, thou tasted of the gall, so weak wert thou made of thy great bleeding.

Against lecherous hearing, that we have grieved thee with, thou would hear with thine ears much wrong ; when men accused thee falsely of sin, shouting out at thy crowning in scorn and hatred, and said, Hail be thou^ king ! and spitted in thy face; the hearing of the foul cry when they all cried, Do him on the rood ! the cross shall be his doom ! and also when they said, He could save other men ; let him save himself now if he can ! By the hearing of these and of other wicked words, thou would in that sweet sense for us be pained.

Against the sin of feeling and of evil goings, thy hands and feet were pierced with hard nails, and from the head to the feet, with crowning and scourging, with buffeting and beating, with spurning and thrusting, with hard cords knitting, and on the cross straining, thou would, glorious Lord, for me be hard pained. There hanged thou so poor and so woe-begone, that of all this world's goods, that were all thine own, thou had 60

[The Passion of Jesus

nought but a poor cloth to eover thy limbs. Thou that art King of kings and Lord of lords—hell and heaven and all this world are all thine own— thou would in time of thy death be so poor for my sake, that thou had not so much earth that thou might die on it; but, on the hard rood, hanging in the air, there was thy deathbed dole fully dight : the rood had a foot of earth, or little more, that it stood upon, and that was to thy pain ! By thee it was sorrowfully said, glorious Lord, that foxes have their dens, and fowls have their nests, but thou at thy death had nothing to rest thy head upon I

Jesu, why is not this the death of me ?—the dolour and the sorrow, when I think in my thought how sorrowfully thou spake when thou said, ttfll ye that pass by this way, stay and behold if ever any pain that ever any suffered, or any worldly woe, be like the sorrow that I suffer for sinful man's sake! Nay, Lord, nay ! there was never none so hard, for it was peerless : of all pains that ever were, was never one found so hard.

And yet thou said, Lord, so sweetly and so
meekly, Vinea mea electa, ego te plantavi, that
is, My dear vineyard, saidst thou (that is, My
dear chosen], have 1 not myself planted thee?

The Passion of Jesus\'7d

Why art thou so bitter ? Popule meus, quid fed tibi ? that is, My sweet, what have I done to thee ? have I angered thee, that thou dost me this woe ? have I not given thee all myself; and all that ever thou hast; and life without end, if thou wilt take it; my body for thy food; and myself to death on the rood ; and promised thee all myself in heaven, for thy meed ? Have I with my good deed hurt thee so sore, or with my sweet persuasion grieved thine heart ?

Lord, thou besought thy Father in heaven for the foul traitors, the tyrants, the tormentors, that he should forgive them thy death, and all that they trespassed ; and thou said that the wretches wist not what they did : and also to the thief that hanged by thy side, that had done theft ever since he was able, that he should be in bliss with thee that same day. Thou said not that he should have long pain for his sin, but at the first asking that he craved thee mercy, and knew thee for God, and his own trespass, at once thou gave him the grant of grace and mercy, for to be in bliss without any longer delay.

Lord, that art the well of mercy, for thy mercy
say to me that am thy thief what thou said to
him—for I have stolen thy good deeds, and used
thy grace amiss, the wits and the virtues that thou

[The Passion of Jesus

hast lent to me. Thou that wert so gracious and so courteous and so mild to grant him that grace in thy greatest woe ; now that thou art in bliss there is nought that grieveth thee—(but our misdeeds are what hinder thee)—nor art thou dangerous nor strange to seek a boon of, but manifold more gracious ; for seldom do men see any man that is not more gracious in his happiness than in his greatest woe.

Ah ! Lord, thy mother was woe ! and thou for her also was woe ! When she should thee forego, and thou took thy leave, entrusting her to saint John as her son instead of thee to serve and care for her: in token of it thou said, Woman, behold thy son! and to John, Behold thy mother! Thou entrusted to a maiden a maiden to keep : thy wisdom would not leave thy mother by herself, but that there should be one assigned to her for comfort.

Ah ! Lady, woe was thee when thou heard that word in thine heart ! that sorrow might have been thy death,—the sorrow of that leave-taking and of thy son's woe. The tears of thine eyes ran full fast, thy sighings and thy sorrows rested full nigh to thy heart ; thou fell down sorrowing, with all thy limbs relaxed ; thine arms fell beside thee ; thine head hanged down ; thy colour waxed

The Passion of Jesus]

full wan, thy face dead-pale : the sword of thy son's woe struck through thine heart. ^Ammam tuam pertransibit gladius: that is, the sword shall glide through thine heart.

Ah! Lady, no tongue may tell that sorrow that thou suffered there at that same exchange ; when thou should take another instead of thy son, thy flesh and thy blood ; a mortal man for almighty God, a disciple for the master, John for Jesus Christ : that exchange was as doleful to thee as a death-throe. Lady, why had I not been by then, and heard what thou heard, and seen that same sight, and taken my part of thy much sorrow, if I might perchance have slaked thy woe ? For men say so,—that it is often solace to have company in pain.

Lord, after that, thou cried so dolefully on the rood, and said that thou thirsted—as was little wonder. Then to thee was given to drink vinegar and gall, by them for whose sake thou would bleed thine heart-blood.

Ah Lord, thou took it and tasted thereof; for thou would be pained for us in each sense. That thirst was two-fold ; in body and in soul. Thou thirsted with a great yearning after the amendment of them that did thee to death, and also for the souls that were then in hell, that had in their

[The Passion of Jesus

lives kept thy laws. Blessed is that same man, glorious Lord, sweet Jesu, that may suffer any thing in his life for thy sake, of bodily pain or any world's shame ; or, for the love of thy name wholly forsake any fleshly lust, ghostly or bodily ; or may in any point follow thee with the shadow of the cross—that is, sharp living.

Ah ! Lord, the pity, the deadly dolour that ought to sink into many hearts, when that men think on that word that thou said on the rood, and to the Father so ruefully made thy moan ; E/oy t E/oy, Lamazabatani: that is, My God^ my dear God, why hast thou altogether forsaken me y that thou sparest me nothing ?

Glorious Lord, thy manhood for us was all-forsaken ; so vile a death and painful never man suffered. Thy Godhead willed it for sinful man's sake, without any sparing of thee that was so woe begone : never was martyrdom nor bodily pain like thine ! Thy manhood was so tender, both bodily and ghostly ; and the pain nevertheless above all pains ! The dignity so excellent, the Father's Son, of heaven ! between two thieves thou hanged on the cross, and that in mid-world — it was no privy shame. As the chieftain of all thieves, in the midst of them thou hanged all naked

; thy skin drawn asunder, and each limb
 The Passion of Jesus]
from other ; the sharp crown on thine head that thou was crowned with ! Thy wounds were so dreadful and so wide-drawn ; the blood that thou bled was doleful to see. The sorrows of thy mother was to thee more pain than all bodily woe ; that surpassed all other : the loss of men's souls that pained thee so !

Lord, of thy much mercy heart may not think, nor that endless love and lovely pity that thou settest on the good that follow thy will : when thy sorrow was so much for them that were thy foes.

Lord, I will in my heart take the rood-foot in mine arms, as thou lay there flat upon the ground with the stench of the dead men's bones that lay there, so dreadful under thy nostrils : nothing shall grieve me then nor change mine heart, so that it shall be to me for great comfort with happy thought. I will not upward cast a glance to see that glorious sight, thy wounds to behold : for, glorious Lord, I am manifold guilty, and the cause thereof, and am unworthy to see that sight.

I would lay me flat on the ground among the
dead, that lie there so foul, and, to keep the
virtue and the grace of thy blood, never will I
thence rise nor go any whither till with thy
[The Passion of Jesus
precious blood I become all red, till I be marked therewith as one of thine own, and my soul be softened in that sweet blood. So may it come to pass, glorious Lord, that mine hard heart may open therewith, that is now hard as stone, be coming all soft and quick in the feeling.

Lord, thy sweet passion raised the dead out 01 their graves, and they walked about; it opened hell-gates ; the earth trembled therewith ; the sun lost his light ; and my sorry heart, that is of the devil's kin, harder than the stone that clove at thy death, cannot feel one little point of thy passion, nor do I rise with the dead in pity of it, nor am I rent as the temple, nor tremble as the earth, nor open the gates that are so hard fastened !

My Lord, is now the malice of my evil heart more than the virtue of thy precious death that wrought such wonders and many an one more— and the memory thereof stirreth not my heart ? Why, Lord, a drop of thy blood to drop on my soul in mind of thy passion may heal all my sore, supple and soften in thy grace what is so hard—and so to die when thy will is.

I wot well, glorious Lord, that my heart is not worthy for thee to come and lie therein ; it is not of the dignity of thine holy sepulchre in
 The Passion of Jesus]
which, in thy manhood, thou were enclosed ; but, Lord, thou lighted to hell, to visit and to set it right; and in that same manner I ask thee to come.

I know well, glorious Lord, that I was never worthy to be thy mother's companion, to stand at thy passion with her and with John ; but, Lord, if in that manner I may not be there for my great unworthiness to see that holy sight, yet I hold me worthy for my great trespass to hang by thy side as the thief hanged. So, Lord, if in virtue of my worthiness I may not be there, I ask in virtue of my guilt to share thy death ; so that though I be not worthy that my heart be visited, yet my need and my wickedness ask that thou set it right.

Come then, at thy will, heavenly physician, and visit me so soon as thou knowest my need ; kindle in my heart a spark of thy passion, of love and of pity» to quicken it with j so that all-burn ing in love above everything, I may forget all the world and bathe me in thy blood. Then shall I bless the time that I feel me so stirred by thy grace, that all worldly weal and fleshly liking contrary to the thought of thy death pleasure me not.

When, Lord, thou had committed into thy Father's hands, at the point of death, thy glorious spirit, and said, Pater in manus tuas, &fV., that is, Father, into thine hands I commit my soul; then, in true tokening of our souls' healing, that all was fulfilled in the bliss of thy blood, thou saidest at the last, Consummatum est, that is, All is ended. Then fell down thine head, and the spirit went out. Then the earth trembled; the sun lost his light; so that all-mirk was the weather, as it had been night; the dead rose, in witness that they knew the Godhead; then the temple was cloven, the rocks were riven. With a sharp spear they struck thine heart; the blood and the water went out thereof.

Thus, glorious Lord, it stirreth in my mind: I see thy blood pour out of hands and of feet, thy side pierced with the spear, thy wounds dried and all run out, thy body all be-bled, thy chin hanging down and thy teeth bare; th? white of thine eyes is cast upward, thy skin that was so lovely is become all pale, the crown on thine head is fearful in my sight, the hair is clotted with the blood and bloweth all about.—The memory of that matter, I would it were my death!

Lord, I see thy mother stand by thy side; she sobbeth and sigheth and falleth down: John on the other side is so full of sorrow. They wring their hands and make much dole. When they look upward the sight of the rood pierceth to their hearts, as it were death. They fall down, weeping and groaning full sore—and I am reason of every woe.

Lady, for thy mercy, since I deserved all that befell thee, and all is my right; grant me, of thy grace, a sight of thy sorrow, a particle of thy pain to occupy me with, that I may in a particle feel somewhat, and a part of thy sorrow—all of which I have made!

Ah! Lord, they cast lots on thy clothes (as the Book said long before), and left thee naked between two thieves; so foul as thy death was, never man suffered. Then began the folk to flock toward the town from the mount of Calvary where thou hanged on the rood. That sight is so wonderful, they flowed so thick, each man to his own home, each his own way. Then was thou in thy Godhead full swiftly at hell, to glad the souls that looked for thy coming. The bliss and the gladdening, the mirth and the liking, that they then had, no man may tell with tongue! Thou opened hell-gates, Lord, through thy might, and took out of pain many that were there;—Adam and Eve, and all that were dear to thee, that had in their lives kept thy laws.

Lord, after that, Joseph of Arimathy took leave of Pilate to take thee down, as it were at time of evensong, with help of Nicodemus, of thy mother and of John, that stood there sorrowfully. They took thy blessed body off the rood, they straightened thine arms that were become stark, and stretched them down by thy sides. They bare thee to the place that thou were buried in; they washed off the cold blood and made thee clean; they laid thee in the sepulchre that was new, that Joseph had ordained for himself; they anointed thee with ointment that smelled sweet. The sorrow that thy mother had, is sorrow indeed to hear!

Lady, the tears that there thou wept, made thy breast and thy cheeks all wet. Thou fell down at his feet, and kissed them full sweet, and ever, as thou kissed, sore thou wept!

Then was there ward set of armed knights, to keep the sepulchre till the third day, &c. Amen. Jesu.

Explicit quaedam meditatio Ricardi Heremitae de Hampole, de passione domini · f>iii

obiit anno
domini

(Here endeth the meditation of Richard, Her mit of Hampole, on the passion of the Lord : who died in the year of the Lord 1348, &c.)

The Passion of Jesus]

sbon$ to Resits anft jftlarg m ti)e

O WEET Jesu, now will I sing

To thee a song of love-longing ; Make in mine heart a well to spring Thee to love above all thing.

Sweet Jesu, mine heart's true light, Thou art day withouten night ; Give to me both grace and might That so I may love thee aright.

Sweet Jesu, my master good, For me thou shedd'st thy blessed blood ; Out of thine heart it came, a flood ; Thy mother saw it with mournful mood,

Sweet Jesu, of my soul the food, All the works of thee be good ; Thou boughtest me upon the rood, And thereon sheddedst thy sweet blood. 72

[The Passion of Jesus

Sweet Jesu, thou child the best, Thy love in mine heart make fast; When I go north, south, east or west, In thee alonely find I rest.

Sweet Jesu, well shall he be That thee in thine own bliss shall see ; With cords of love do thou draw me That I may come and dwell with thee.

Sweet Jesu, thou heavenly king, Best and fairest of all thing : Bring me to that love-longing, To come to thee at mine ending.

Jesu, to thy disciples dear

Thou saidest with full mournful cheer

As they were sitting all a-fear,

A little ere thou taken were—

Jesu, thou saidest that thou were Full of sorrow and heart-sore, And bade them bide a little there While thou besought thy Father's ear. 73

The Passion of Jesus]

To him thou said'st, If it may be, My Father dear, I pray to thee, May this pain pass away from me ! But as thou wilt, so may it be !

Jesu, with that thou prayed again ; The sweat of blood from thee down-ran ; From heaven an angel lighted then To comfort thee both God and man.

Jesu, for love thou sufFredst wrong, Wounds very sore and torments strong ; How rueful were thy pains and long I may not tell in spell no' song.

Jesu, thy crown pressed on thee sore ! The scourging when thou scourged were ! It was for me—Ah ! Jesu, hear !— The pains that thou didst suffer there !

Jesu, most sweet, thou hanged on tree Not for thy guilt but all for me ; For sins and guilt they injured thee : Ah ! Jesu sweet, forgive thou me !

[The Pass ton of Jesus

Jesu, when thou all strained were, Thy pains they waxed more and more. Thy mother aye with thee was there, With sighings sorrowful and sore.

Jesu, what didst thou see in me Of aught that needful was to thee, That thou so hardly on rood-tree For me, a wretch, would pained be ?

Jesu, my love, thou art so free That all thou didst for love of me : What can I render back to thee ? Thou heedest but the love of me !

Jesu, my God, my Lord, my King, Thou askest me none other thing But my true love and heart's longing And loving tears and still mourning.

Jesu, my dear, my love, my light, I will love thee, and that is right. Make me love thee with all my might And after thee mourn day and night. 75

The Passion of j[esus]

Mary, Lady, Mother bright! Thou canst! thou wilt! thou art of might Love of my heart, my life, my light! Pray thou for me both day and night!

Jesu, although I sinful be, Full long time hast thou spared me : The more then ought I to love thee, Since thou with me hast been so free.

Jesu, of love I see tok'ning ; Thine arms outspread to love-clasping ; Thine head bowed down to sweet kissing Open thy side to love-shewing ;

Mary, I pray, as thou art free, Of thy sorrow to share with me, That I may sorrow here with thee And partner of thy bliss may be.

Jesu, thou saidest, O alt ye That pass along the way by me, A while abide ye, come and see If any sorrow is like to me.

[The Passion of Jesus

Jesu, thou saidest, Tell thou me. My dearest folk, what may it be That I have so offended thee. That thou so bitter art to me ?

Mary, thou that slak'st all woe Hell-pains do thou shield me fro* And give me grace here to do so That I from hence to heaven go.

Jesu, my Lord, mine own sweeting Hold me ever in thy keeping : Make of me thine own darling, That I love thee above all thing.

Jesu, what is fair to see, What to fleshly ease may be, All the world's bliss, make me flee; And all my mind to give to thee.

Mary, thou sweet maiden free, By Jesu Christ beseech I thee, Make thou thy sweet son love me; And make me worthy that so it be.

The Passion of Jesus]

Jesu, if thou forsakest me, What can please of all I see ? For bliss may not within me be Until thou come again to me.

Jesu, my soul is wed to thee; By right it ought thine own to be; Though I have sinn'd so against thee, Thy mercy ready is for me.

Jesu, be thou all my yearning,
In thee be, Lord, all my liking,
My thought, my deed, and my mourning,
To have thee ever in love-longing.
Jesu, my soul it prayeth thee,
Let it not unclothed be ;
Clothe it with thine own love free,
With such good works as pleasure thee.

Jesu, for beauty ask I not, Nor for proud clothing nobly wrought, Lands nor rentals, dearly bought— But hearty love and cleanly thought,

The Passion of Jesus

Mary, thy son pray heartily For me, a wretch, all unworthy That he will vouchsafe wholly To grant to me his great mercy.

Jesu, grant that I may see The much of good thou hast done me : And I unkind again have been ! Forgive me, Lord, that art so free.

Jesu, thy love and fleshly thought Dwell together, can they not : As honey and gall together brought, Sweet and bitter, accordeth not.

Jesu, though I be unworthy Thee to love, Lord almighty, Thy goodness maketh me hardy, My soul to set in thy mercy.

Jesu, thy mercy comforts me ; For no man may so sinful be If he leave sin and flee to thee ? But mercy ready findeth he,

The Passion of Jesus]

Jesu, though I so sinful be, I ever trust and hope in thee, Therefore, Lord, I pray to thee That of my sins amend thou me,

Mary mild, full of pity, Pray to thy dear son for me, That he may grant me to be Ever in bliss with him and thee.

Jesu, make me do thy will Now and ever, loud and still: With thy love my soul fulfil, And suffer ne'er that I do ill.

Jesu, if thou from me dost go Mine heart is full of pain and woe What may I say but IVfll-a-woe ! When thou, my sweet, art gone me fro* ?

Jesu, my lite, my Lord, my King! To thee my soul hath great longing, Thou hast it wedded with thy ring ; When thy will is, to thee it bring !

[Tie Passion of Jesus

Jcsu, all fair, my lover bright! I thee beseech with all my might, Bring my soul into thy light, Where all is day and never night.

Jesu, help thou at mine ending; Take my soul at my dying ; Send it succour and comforting; That it dread no wicked thing.

Jesu, thy bliss hath no ending, There is no sorrow and no weeping, But peace and joy with great liking : Sweet Jesu, us thereto bring ! Amen.

(Whoso oft saith this with good will Shall find God's grace his love to fill; The Holy Ghost his heart shall till, Save him from sin and from fiend*s ill.)

The Passion of Jesut]

0 imitation of ti)e jpibe ^Sounfcs of gjmis Cjw*t

BEHOLD especially the five most notable wounds, two in his blessed hands, and two in his blessed feet, and the most open wound in his right side.

Into these wounds of Christ's blessed hands and feet (with Thomas of India) put in thy fingers,—that is to say, thy most subtle thoughts and desires.

And in the wound of Christ's blessed side, since it is the largest and deepest, put in all thine hand, —that is to say, all tny love and all thy works; and there feel Christ s heart so hot, loving thee ; and there feel Christ's blessed heart-blood shed for thee and to ransom thy soul; also there feel the water of Christ s side streaming out, as of a well of life, for to wash thee and all mankind of sin.

And then seize up water of everlasting life

[The Passion ofjesus

without end out of these five most open wounds of Christ, as out of five well-springs.

And understand, see and behold and learn, that the wound in Christ's right hand is the well of wisdom: the wound in Christ's left hand is the well of mercy : the wound in Christ's right foot is the well of grace : the wound in Christ's left foot is the well of ghostly comfort: the largest and deepest wound, the which is in Christ's right side, is the well of everlasting life.

Out of the well of wisdom in Christ's right hand, seize up the wholesome water of true learn ing and teaching. Learn there how much Christ, God and man, loved man's soul; and how precious is man's soul ; for, because of his great love of man's soul, Christ Jesu (that is, the wisdom of the Father of heaven), should and would, by the ordinance of the blessed Trinity, suffer his righteous right hand so dispiteously to be nailed to the cross.

Out of the well of mercy, in Christ's left hand, seize up devoutly the sweet water of remission and forgiveness of our sins ; and learn busily here, for thy salvation, this lesson of mercy. For notwithstanding that the while mankind was enemy to God, yet our blessed Father of heaven spared not his own Son, but suffered him to be stretched on the hard cross, more dispiteously and grievously than ever was sheepskin stretched on the wall or on parchment-maker's harrow to dry against the sun (for it is likely that the blessed arms of Jesu Christ were so sore strained and spread abroad on the cross for love of us, that the veins burst). Learn here then, in this well of mercy in Christ's left hand (in whose left hand, hanging and wielding, be all riches in heaven and in earth), how much is his love, and how great is that flood ever flowing and also springing of his mercy freely proffered to man, that suffered so dreadfully and grievously his blessed arms to be spread and nailed to the cross, to proffer his mercy and himself to us his unkind enemies. Therefore since everlasting good God hath it of nature, of custom and of might, to do mercy that may never cease nor fail (unless God lose his nature, or lose his virtue or lose his might;—but since this may never fail in good God almighty, all knowing and all well-willing) ; therefore trustfully and stedfastly, out of this well of the wound of Christ's left hand, seize up the water of everlasting mercy of Jesu Christ.

Out of the well of grace in Christ's right foot seize up the water of ghostly refreshing, by bethinking thee inwardly what grace of salvation was proffered to us all, in that Christ himself would suffer his right foot so dreadfully to be wounded ; (of the which foot holy writ speaketh that the stool that it treadeth upon is worshipped, for it is holy ;) and so hard to be nailed to the cross that he would never part from thee, unless, at least, thou wilt forsake him. Here thou might lightly seize up water of great grace proffered to us all.

Out of the well of ghostly comfort in Christ's left foot seize up the joyful water of spiritual comfort and gladness ; that the king of bliss loved our souls so heartily that for our salvation he would suffer so sore a wound with that hideous nail through his left foot that was so tender—(for there come together there the veins from Christ's heart)—and thus suffered our blessed Jesu for helping of us. Here we may seize up out of this blessed well water of ghostly comfort and joyful gladness of our souls without end.

Out of the largest and deepest well of everlasting life in the most open wound in Christ's blessed side seize up deepest and heartliest water of joy and bliss without end, beholding there inwardly how Christ Jesu, God and man, to bring thee to everlasting life, suffered that hard and hideous death on the cross, and suffered his side to be opened and himself to be pierced to the heart with that dreadful spear ;—and so with that doleful stroke of the spear there gushed out of Christ's side that blissful flood of water and blood to ransom us, water of his side to wash us, and blood of his heart to buy us.

For love of these blessed wounds creep into this hot bath of Christ's heart-blood, and there bathe thee : for there was never sin of man nor of woman, thought nor wrought, that was laved with lovely sorrow and hearty repentance, that there is not in this well full remission to buy it, and water of life fully to cleanse and wash it.

Therefore rest thee here, comfort thee here, live in Christ's heart without end. Amen.
[The Passion of Jesus
on tije mnbols of

OVERNACLE ! I honour him and thee, That thee made through his privity ; The cloth he set upon his face, The print he left there, of his grace, His mouth, his nose, his eyen too, His beard, his hair,—he did also ; Shield me for all that in my life That I have sinned with senses five, Namely, with mouth of slandering, Of false oaths and of backbiting, And made boast with tongue also, Of all the sins committed too,— Lord of heaven, forgive them me, Through sight of the figure that I here see,

The Passion of Jesus]
Cultellus circumcisionis:
This knife betokeneth circumcision ;
Thus he destroyed sin, all and some,
Of our forefather old Adam
Through whom we nature took of man.
From temptation of lechery
Be my succour when I shall die.

Pellicanus:
The pelican his blood did bleed Therewith his nestlings for to feed : This bctokcncth on the rood How our Lord fed us with his blood, When he us ransomed out of hell In joy and bliss with him to dwell, And be our father and our food, And we his children meek and good. 88
[T/ie Passion of Jesus

Trlginta denarii :
The pence also that Judas told, For which Lord Jesu Christ was sold, Shield us from treason and avarice Therein to perish in no wise.

Lanterna:
The lantern where they bare the light When Christ was taken in the night ; May it light me from nightly sin That I never be seized therein.
The Passion of Jesus]

Gladil et fustes :
Swords and staven that they bare
Jesu Christ therewith to fear ;
From fiends, good Lord, do thou keep me,
Of them afraid that I not be.

Arundines:

Christ was stricken with a reed, With it the Jews did break his head ; With good cheer and mildest mood, All he suffered and still he stood. When I wrong any, or any me, Be it forgiven for that pity 1 QO

[The Passion of Jesus

Manus depillans ft alapans : The hand, O Lord, that tare thy hair, And the hand that clapped thee on the ear, May that pain be my succour there That I have sinned with pride of ear ; And of all other sins also That with mine ears have I hearkened to !

Judaeus spuens in facie Chrhti:

The Jew that spat in God's own face ; For that he suffered, give us grace, What I have reviled, or any me, For that despite, forgiven it be ! 9*

The Passion of Jesus']

Velamen ante oculos:

The cloth before thine eyen too To buffet thee they knit it so; May it preserve me from vengeance, Of childhood and of ignorance And of other sins also, That I have with mine eyes done too, And with my nostrils sins of smell That I have done when sick or well !

Tunica inconsutilis et vestis purpurea :

The garment white that had seam none, The purple they laid lot upon, Be they my succour and my keeping, For my body's use of soft clothing !

[The Passion of Jesus

Virgae et flageuat:

With great reeds thou wert sorely dashed, With scourges painful sorely lashed ; May that pain rid me of sins these, Namely, of sloth and idleness !

Corona spinea :

The crown of thorn, on thine head thrust, That tare thine hair, and thy skin buist, Shield me from hell-pit's agony That I deserve through my folly 1

The Passion of Jesus]

Columna cum corda :
To the pillar, Lord, also
With a rope they bound thee too ;
The sinews from the bones did burst
So hard 'twas drawn and strained fast;
That bond release me and unbind
Of that I've trespassed and been unkind !

Christ us for tans crucem in humero :

The cross behind on his backbone, That he suffered death upon, Give me grace while yet I live Clean of sin me for to shrive, And thereto give true penitence, And to fulfil here my penance ! 94

[The Passion of yes us

Vestigia sahatoris, quando exivit per port am Jerusalem, portando crucem, corona?n spineam coronatus, mille passus sic incedens^ roseum cruorem distillanao :

Thou bare the cross and took thy gait Out of Jerusalem's city-gate ; All thy footsteps sweet and good Were seen through shedding of thy blood ; Thou met with women of Bethlehem And also of Jerusalem, And all wept for thine agony ; To them thou saidest openly : Now weep ye not for this my woe y Hut for your children weep also ; For them ye may lament full sore. And your salt tears for them down pour $ For they shall Jiave great torment hard An hundred winters here-afterward. Those steps of thine give us pardon When forth we go with devotion On pilgrimage on horse or foot, Of all our sins be they our boot ! » * Help. 95

The Passion of Jesus]

Clam:

The nails through feet and hands also, Help they me out of sin and woe That I have here in my life done, With hands handled, or on feet gone !

Malleus:

The hammer, Lord, both stern and great, That drove the nails through hands and feet, Be it my succour in my life If any smite me with staff or knife !

[The Passion of Jesus

Vas cum felle :

The vessel with vinegar and gall May it keep me from the sins all That to the soul are venom dread, That thereby I be not poisoned !

Spongea :

Though thou thirsted sore withal They gave thee vinegar and gall; From what I have drunken in gluttony May it save me when I shall die ; That, Lord, now I pray to thee For that grievance thou suffered for me 97 O

The Passion of Jesus]

Lancea:

Lord, that spear so sharply ground, Within thy heart which made a wound. Quench the sin that I have wrought, Or in my heart have evil thought, And of my stout pride thereto, And mine unbuxomness also !

Scaa :

The ladder set up by occasion
When thou wert dead to be taken down,
When I am dead in any sin
me that I die not therein ! 98

[The Passion of Jesus

Forceps :

The tongs that drew the sharp nails out Of feet and hands and all about, And loosed thy body from the tree, Of all my sins may they loose me '

Sepulchrum Christi:
The sepulchre wherein was laid His blessed body all be-bled, May he send me ere that I die Sorrow of heart and tear or eye, Clear and cleansed that I be, Ere to my grave I betake me ! So that I may on the Doomsday To judgment come without dismay^

The Passion of Jesus]
And wend to bliss in company
Wherein a man shall never die,
But dwell in joy with our Lord right;
There is aye day and never night,
That ever lasts withouten end :—
Now Jfsu Christ us thither send ! Amen.
[The Passion of Jesus
Example of tfte passion
" See what our Lord suffered for our sake "
TDOTH young and old, where'er ye be, " In Jesu's name good cheer ye make ! And lift ye up your hearts and see
What our Lord suffered for our sake. As meek as any lamb was he,
Ensample of him may we take, To suffer too in our degree
And in his service aye to wake.
And if our friends forsake us here,
So that we be all alone, Think we on Christ that bought us dear,
And to him make all our moan : For of that Lord well may we learn
What wrong he suffered among his foen ; When his disciples fled for fear,
There 'bode no more but Mary and John. 101
The Passion of Jesus]
If any wrong to us be wrought,
Be it in word or else in deed, Be of good cheer yet at the thought
How God may help us all at need : Think we how Jesus Christ us bought,
And for our sins his blood did bleed ; For his own sinning was it not,
For he did never sinful deed.
If wicked men do us defame,
Think we how Christ was bought and sold ; For him to suffer is no shame,
But him to serve look we be bold. And if men injure our good name,
We must forgive, both young and old 5 For though we suffer so much blame
Christ suffered more a thousandfold.
Of poverty if we complain,
For that we lack some worldly good ; Think we on Jesu that Lord Sov'reign,
How poor he hung upon the rood : And how he strived not again,
But ever was meek and mild of mood ; To follow that Lord we should be fain,
In what degree that e'er we stood. 102
[The Passion of Jesus
And though we have sorrow on each side,

And all about us wrong and woe, Yet suffer meekly, and abide
And think on Christ that suffered also ; And how he was in full great dread,
Unto his pains when he should go : He suffered more in his man-head
Than ever did man or ever shall do.
Though we with wrong to death be brought,
Yet suffering is the surest way ; For love of Jesu that us dear bought,
And died for us on Good-Friday ; So think we therefore in our thought
That we our Lord should please and pay, And learn to set this world at nought,
And suffer wicked men to say.
In Jesu Christ was meekness most ;
And therefore he the mastery had, And bound the fiend for all his boast,
That never was he so sore a-dread ; Against his will and all his host
Adam and Eve with him he led, And many more from out that coast
That were in prison full hard bestead. 103

The Passion of Jesus]

If thou in Jesu have delight
Though all the world do thee assail, Do after this ; and thou shalt wit
That meekness will thee most avail: For whoso sufPreth here despite,
And meekly abideth in that battail, It will turn them to great profit,
And endless joy for their travail.
If any do to us amiss,
Or us in any wise offend, For love of Jesu have mind on this,
And let meekness thy mood amend With Jesu Christ, as one of his,
And suffer meekly what God shall send ; Then shall we be with him in bliss
That aye shall last withouten end. Amen.

[The Passion of Jesus

jlilttittation on t&e passion . . . anfc on si nobs of

PEN thine heart with sigh ings sore to think on the pains that Jesus Christ suffered ; and set them in thy soul, in order as he suffered them.

How they defiled his holy face with spitting ; how they buffeted the fairest face of all man kind ; how with cords they bound his fair hands, so that out of all his fingers the blood outburst ; how they beat him with knotted scourges ; how all with one voice cried, Do him on cross, that he die as shameful a death as ever any died , how he was stretched on the cross that was laid on the earth ; and drawn out with ropes, till they make hands and feet accord with the holes that were made in the tree. So strait was he drawn out on the cross that men might tell all his bones ; and to that cross was he fastened with iron nails.

Think after how his body was lifted up with the cross and smitten oft into the earth (as men do a stake of a tree to make it to stand fast), 105

The Passion of Jesus']

with that sweet living body that hanged thereon ! At this smiting into the earth all his veins burst, so that out of all his sweet limbs the blood out streamed. This grieved him sorest of all other pains, except our unkindness that every day renews his pain.

Think after how knights kneeled to him, and said to him in scorn, Hail, king of Jews! Thou that helpest many, thou needest now help thy self; come down from the cross that thou art nailed to, and we shall trow that thou art God's Son of heaven.

Think on the sharp crown of thorns that made his lovely face all to stream with blood ;

and on the bitter vinegar mingled with gall that they gave him to drink when he complained him of thirst, as he had bled so much. But, wit thou well, he thirsts not after spiced drink nor wine nor after any other liquor, but only after the love of men that he so dearly bought. Think then, when thou dost anything against his will, that thou dost as the Jews did—thou givest him gall to drink, as an unkind wretch !

Think on his care-full mother, and on saint John his dear cousin, that stood by him and saw all that he suffered ; no tongue may tell how sorry they were at that time.

[The Passion of Jesus

Think on the words he spake to his mother, hanging on the rood, Woman^ lo ! here thy son ! to saint John his cousin, Lo ! here thy mother dear ! Serve thou her with all thy might. What sighings came to her heart when she heard his words, when man's son for God's Son, the disciple for the master, the servant for the lord, was given to tend her.

Think on that blessed body, naked and pale, hanging on the rood, so riven with scourges that naught was left whole. And yet so poorly was he furnished in that struggle that he had naught to rest his head on ; and as naked as he was born, save for his mother's kerchief knit about his limbs.

Think how full he was of mercy while yet he hanged on rood, who forgave his sins to the thief that hanged beside him, and that had mis-called him a while before, and promised him that he should be with him that day in paradise.

When thou art bethinking thee of all the pains that Jesus suffered for thee, think in thy soul that thou standest by him in that place and seest what they do to him : speak then to thy Lord the words of saint Bernard : God, my Lord> sweet Jesu, what hast thou done that thou so bloody hangest on rood, thou that never did evil, but ever

The Passion of Jesus]

did good? Thee guiltless, they do to death : woe is me therefore^ for 1 am guilty of thy death ! and it is against law and reason to slay him that never did amiss, and let him go free that did the harm Therefore ye wretches, ye Jews, take me, for I am the sinful one that has done evil and followed the fiend's counsel. I pray you let this Innocent pass, and do me to death, for I have trespassed !

Think also inwardly how he said on the rood before he yielded up the ghost—for it may stir thee to have sorrow for thy sins, and pity for his death that was so pained for thee, and so wreak his death on thyself—that he thus on the rood cried, Consummatum est; that is, All is ful filled ; as if he said, / am fulfilled of sorrow both in body and sou. In body, for all was pained from the crown of the head to the sole of the foot: in soul, through our unkindness, that gave him no thanks for his good deed, but who ever do what in us is to renew his pain ;—and that overpasses all his pains that he suffered before. Therefore he said at his end, am fulfilled of sorrow ; and at this word he bowed down his head and said to his Father, Into thy hands my soul I yield.

Think then on the wonders that then befell ; how creatures that had no wit sorrowed at his death. The sun withdrew his brightness and

[772 Passion of Jesus

became all mirk, and thus shewed that it sor rowed for Christ's death ; the hard rock was riven ; the earth quaked ; the graves opened, and the dead men that were in them rose to life and witnessed that he was very God that the Jews did to death, with sighings and tears.

Also I counsel that thou think on the piercing sorrows of his mother that was with him aye till he died, and beheld all that they did with her child. Never suffered martyr so much as she suffered ; for the martyrs were pained in body, and God's mother in soul that may not die ; for all the pains that her son suffered pierced through her soul, and she yearned to die for sorrow, and no sorrow might slay her. Then was fulfilled the word of Simeon : Tuam ipsius animam pertransibit gladius; that is, The sword of sorrow shall pierce through thy soul.

Think also inwardly what he is that thus suffered, and how unworthy they were to be loved for whom he died. For if thou have oft in mind these thoughts, they will hold thy heart in love, and make thee to flee sin.

Think after with what devotion he was taken down off the rood ; how the three Maries dight him with ointments and wrapped his body in white clothes and laid him in a tomb of rock.

The Passion of yesus]

Think after of his wending to hell ; what comfort they had that so long abode his coming, there in mirk state ; what sorrow and dread, sighing and gnashing, the fiends of hell had at that time; how he bound Satan so that he might never thereafter harm nor offend the folk as before.

After of his up-rising, how bright, how fair he rose in body that the Jews so loathely treated in intent for to have destroyed the memory of him for ever : and now he lives almighty God and king, crowned in heaven, and shall judge them at his will.

Think what joy all his disciples had when they saw him risen and to have the mastery of death : before, they denied him and said they knew him not, but then they repented that they had mis-said, and loved him as their Lord, and were so filled full of his love that they were ready to die for him, and requite him death for death.

To tell what joy his mother had when she saw him risen to life,—no man may tell.

Think after how he ascended to heaven with our manhood, and set it on the right hand of almighty God his Father, and so fastened our nature in himself that they shall never part ; and through this union, if we keep us from sin ? HQ

The Passion of Jesus

or repent and shrive us of that we have mis-done, and turn no more again, we may claim as heirs to dwell in his bliss.

Think that he shall come and judge all man kind, and give to each man according as he has wrought ; and as gladful as his coming is to the good, so aweful and dreadful shall it be to the evil.

For God threatens the evil with THREE ARROWS and says, Congregabo super eos mala^ et sagittas tres complebo in els ; that is, / shall heap on them all kinds of evil and woe, and my three sharp arrows shall I fasten in them, that shall so wound the sinful that he shall never recover.

The FIRST ARROW is when he shall bid them rise and come to their doom with these words : Surgite mortui, venite ad judicium ; that is, Rise^ ye that are dead, and come to your doom. Through might of these words all that were dead shall quicken. This is the arrow of which saint Jerome said, Sive comedam, sive bibam, semper videtur mihi quod ilia vox terribilis insonet auribus meis, Surgite mortui^ venite ad judicium ; that is, Whether I eat or drink or whatever else I do, ever I think these dreadful words ring in mine ill

The Passion of Jesus]

ears, Rise, ye that are dead, and come to your doom. Since this holy man dreaded these words, need is a sinful man should dread them, lest he fall in sin. For Solomon says, Sicut fremitus leonis, it a via ejus ; that is, The vengeance of the judge at his coming is^&s the roaring of a lion. The lion's nature is to fright all beasts with his roaring, and yet dare they not flee : and though this noise be dreadful to all beasts, yet it comforteth his own whelps and quickens them to life. So shall Jesu Christ at the strait judgment do to all beast-like men that have lived in sin and would make no ending of their ill: at this calling shall they be so frighted and so un-mighty, that on no side can they flee, but they shall remain, and receive as they have seived. And as he shall be wrathful to these wretches, so shall he be lovely to his own children that have wrought his will here ; for they shall waken with joy at his calling, and wend with him to dwell in bliss.

But the sinful wretches shall seek to hide them, that they see not his dreadful face that frights them out of their wit : as Ysalah says, Introibunt in cavernas petrarum et voragines terrae a facie formidinis Domini; cum surrexit percutere terram^ that is, The cursed and tinful

[The Passion of Jesus

men shall creep into the crevices of the rocks and into holes in the earth, for to hide them from the vengeful face of God when he rises to smite the earth, —that is, when he shall come to judge men on earth. Of this coming speaketh Anselm and says, On one side shall our sins bitterly accuse us of the slaughter of our soul. On another side shall stand righteousness wherewith is no pity. Above us the avenging judge, that is as wrathful there as he is tender here ; mild here, stern there ; and he is both judge and witness that knows all our guilt.

The SECOND ARROW is when God arraigns them of all that they have mis-done since they were born ; and the judge shall shew his wounds to all men, that they may see truly what he, the unguilty, bore for their sins ; and with this word shall he arraign them.

Of the earth I took thee, and with my hands made thee, in paradise that lovely place, there with out care to have dwelled, if thou had been buxom to me and kept my commandment: but soon thou brake it, and left me for mine enemy. Therefore righteous* ness damned thee to hell, there to be in sorrow and woe. When I saw afterwards thine evil plight, 1 had pity on thee, though thou deserved none. 1 113 H

The Passion of Jesus]

lighted to earth and took thy nature, where I was sore pained and despised ; and I took for thee much villainy in deed and word. And after Judas had sold me, the Jews took me and buffeted me and spit in my face; with sharp thorns they crowned me ; with knotted scourges they beat me; so loathely they treated me that I was like a leper to look upon. Ah this ought to have made thee have pity on me if thou had been kind. In my thirst they gave me to drink vinegar mingled with bitter gall; they pierced my feet and hands ; and nailed me to the rood; and opened my side with a spear, and made my heart to bleed. I forgat myself, for on thee was all my thought ; and yet thou, as an unkind man, settest all at nought f

Now, thou unkind man, understand and look to me, and behold my side, feet and hands, how woeful I am made for thee, and to heal thy wounds : and therefore thou should have loved me the more : for I wot not what more I might have done for thee than I have done. Therefore need behoves thee to shew what thou have done or suffered for me ; for now my righteousness wills that I fashion for each man his meed, to dwell for ever in pain or in joy, according as he has served.

How then shall fare the cursed sinful man when he is thus arraigned of the wrathful judge,

[The Passion of Jesus

and all his sins shewed to all men ? For nought may there be hid ; save that which was done with here—with shrift. For holy Job says, Revelabunt caeli iniquitatem ejus, et terra consurget adversus eum ; that is, Heaven shall shew the wickedness of the sinful, and earth shall rise ana stand against him and bear witness of his works. And further the apostle says,

Testimonium red-det illis conscientia eorum; that is, Their con-science shall bear witness against the sinful, from the which man may not hide. And further his evil works shall stand by him at the dreadful judg ment, and bitterly strive with him and say, We are the works that thou, wretched man, has wrought in despite of thy good Lord ; for thou wrought us against his will, that shed his heart-blood for thee. Now it repenteth thee that ever thou sinned; but, sorry wretch, all too late ! And therefore shall we dwell with thee without end for to increase thy pain.

The THIRD ARROW shall he shoot when he says these words, Ite maledicti in ignem aeternum; that is, Go ye cursed into endless fire !

The holy man says, The eyes of those that are in that fire and smoke shall weep more tears than there is water in the broad sea. This fire, as saint Austin says, burns so fiercely and ever the

"5

The Passion of Jesus]

same, and is so mighty in its nature, that though all this world's waters all overflowed it, it might not slacken nor cool this fire at all. This fire aye maketh smoke, that maketh the wretches to weep ; and their tears strengthen the fire that is there, as oil would, if it were cast in the fire here. The holy man had mind of these tears, that said to his disciples when they had long cried on him to say them some good word,— My dear chll-dren^ he said, weep we here ! so that our tears seek us not in hell!

When the cursed man hears and wits that he is damned, and wits there is no returning nor mercy to find, then he says the words of Job, Oh that the day might perish in which I was born and the night in which I was conceived! Why died I not In my mother's wo?nb ? Alas! that sorry while that ever I was born ! IVherejore set me my mother on her knee, and washed me and rocked me and fed me at her breast ? Alas ! the day ! So much travail she lost that nursed me ! — a brand to smoulder in hell-fire

But God's own children that here have done his will shall be led with angels to the bliss of heaven, there to be in joy ever without end.

So great is that joy, as the apostle tells, that no

[The Passion of Jesus

heart may think it, nor eye see it. If man might be in that joy half-an-hour and feel that heavenly pleasure, and were brought again to this middle earth, so strange pain it were to him to live herein, that, even if all the wealth of this world were at his will, he would his body were torn in a thousand pieces to win that joy again from which he came.

Think thou was with Jesu Christ in all his pains, and that thou stood so near him in all his passion-time and all the hardness that was done to him ; and be a-wondered that so great a Lord would bear such hardness; and fall down to the earth, as guilty of his death, and thank him for the wounds that he bore for thee, and have him ever in mind.

Think not of all this together at one time as they stand in order, for fear of cooling of devotion, but now on one, now on another, as thou feel that God stirs thee of his dear grace.

[Thus many wounds God suffered for mankind; — five thousand and four hundred and sixty and fifteen. And thou shalt say in the whole year as many paternosters^ if thou say cach day of the year fifteen.]

The Passion of Jesus]
£antus Ccmpasstorm

Hie incipiunt cantm compfissionts Christi et con-solationis aeternae*

UNKIND man, give heed to me, And look what pain I bear for thee ! Sinful man, on thee I cry, 'Tis only for thy love I die. Behold the blood from me down runs Not for my guilt, but for thy sins. My hands, my feet with nails are fast, Sinews and veins are wholly burst. The blood that flows from my heart-root, Look ! it falls down to my foot. Of all the pain I suffer sore, Within my heart there grieves me more The unkindness I find in thee, Who for thy love thus hanged on tree. Alas ! why lovest thou me not ? And I thy love so dear have bought ! IKS

[The Passion of Jesus

Save thou love me, thou dost me wrong,

Since I have loved thee so long :

Two-and-thirty year and more

I was for thee in travail sore,

With hunger, thirst, in heat and cold,

For thy love both bought and sold,

Pained, nailed and done on tree,

All, man, for the love of thee !

Love thou me, as well thou may,

And from sin withdraw away.

I give my body with wounds sore ;

And thereto I shall give thee more,

Besides all this, also, I wis,

In earth my grace, in heaven my bliss.

Jesus. Amen

The Passion of Jesus]

O INFUL man, look up and see how ruefully

I hung on rood, And on my penance have pity, with sorrowful

heart and mournful mood, All this, man, I bore for thee ; my flesh was

riven ; all bled my blood ; Lift up thy heart: call tnou on me ; forsake thy

sin j have mercy God!

LO ! sweet beloved, now may thou see That I have lost my life for thee 5 What might I do thee more ? Therefore I pray thee specially That thou forsake ill company That woundeth me so sore.

And take thou mine alms privily, And lay them in thy treasury

In whatever state thou dwells ; And, sweet beloved, forget thou not That I thy love so dear have bought;

And I ask thee nought else I

PART III DEVOTIONS FOR COMMUNION

[Devotions for Communion

ttjk CJUmbrng of out Hold

Here followeth a devout prayer to our Lord Jesu Christ^ with a meditation to be said before the re ceiving of the holy sacrament^ with inward devotion of desire , with meek fear and fervour of love.

KIND Jesu that wouldest suffer so many grievous pains and death for love of man kind, great and marvellous was thy charity, that thou vouchsafedst with thy precious blood to wash our sins.

I pray thee, gracious Lord, that thou forgive me all my sins that I have done, thought and said ; in pride, in wrath, in envy, in covetousness, in gluttony, in sloth, in lechery, in uncleanness of body and soul ; my five senses misused, thy commandments broken, my time of life wasted in vice ; neither have I followed virtue, nor done the good, ghostly and bodily, that I might have done.

Merciful Jesu, with that precious blood that thou sheddedst on the rood-tree for our salvation, wash away all our sins that we have done in our life ; heal and comfort us with the holy sacrament which thou didst ordain and leave here in earth to be our medicine and our life, through which we should live after thee and dwell in thee and thou in us. For, good Lord, thou didst speak of that holy work (which after thou madest and gavest to thine apostles) when thou saidst, The bread that I shall give to you —/'/ is my flesh for the life and restoration of this world. He that worthily receiveth me, he shall live because of me; and he shall dwell with me and I with him. O holy and mightful priest and bishop, who by thy divine might madest the worthy sacrament that is thy precious body in form of bread ; O good Lord Jesu give me grace to receive it this day with purity of heart and cleanness of soul, with love, fear, and stedfast belief. O kind Jesu, I wot well and I confess to thy high majesty that I am not worthy to come to thy board to be fed with so royal meat as is thy blessed body, that is very God and man. For, good Lord, how might I presume to receive or touch thee, whom Peter the prince of the apostles put from him with meek fear, saying thus, Go from me, Lord^ for I am a sinful man ? Also, Lord, saint John the Baptist that was hallowed in his mother's womb, and, even after that, holy and perfect in living, yet he trembled and quaked for fear of his great unworthiness, when he should baptize and touch Christ. And also, Lord, the centurion said, Lord, I am not worthy that thou shouldst enter into my house.

Who is there then, that may make him ready, or prepare him worthily for so great mysteries ? O good Lord, among all those that ever were born of woman there is never an one who might of his own strength only, or of the righteousness of his works, sufficiently prepare him to receive thee, even were it that a man had the natural cleanness of all angels, or all the brightness of glorified saints, or all the merits of holy lives on earth, by straitness of perfect living : For all these, without the special grace of thee, my Lord God, are not able nor worthy to receive so great mysteries as is thy holy sacrament.

O thou everlasting and almighty God, how dreadful, how sorrowful it is to me, that I am a sinner ! Alas ! alas ! good Lord; mercy ! mercy! mercy ! since the angels be not clean in thy sight, and men of great works be not worthy by their own righteousness to receive thee ; O thou good gracious Lord, what shall befall me that have wallowed every day in the filth of the clay of sins, and have little or nought of devotion, nor be, as should be, grieved for my wretched sins and great negligences.

Ah ! dear Lord, what fear is this to me, that I may come worthily to this sacrament!

And, truly, Lord, I may fear lest what should be to me for forgiveness, turn into a sorrowful fall. But, gracious Lord, this again alone comforteth me, that this sacrament of thine endless pity is ordained for a remedy against sin. And therefore I will do what in me is, fitting me for thy holy grace. And, Lord, thou asleest not of me what thou sayest is impossible for me. And thou wilt not the death of a sinner, but that he turn and live ; and thou earnest down unto this earth for sinners. And, Lord, I hope I am one of those that thou earnest for, and therefore trusting in thy great pity and endless mercy, I, that am sick through sin, draw near to thee, Lord, that art the physician for sin. And I that am spiritually hungry for lack of grace, come to thee, Lord, that art the well of mercy. And I that am needy and poor, desire thee that art king of heaven and of earth, and hast all in thy power. And I that am dry and barren and would be sorrowful for all my sins, covet thee, Lord, which art all sweetness

and comfort and endless bliss and sovereign will, to deliver me of my sin. And, gracious Lord, I believe verily that thou canst make me worthy and fit for thy grace, that madest all things of nought by thy divine might, and of what was sinful hast made rightful and holy in a moment of time.

Ah ! gracious Lord, in worship of these graces and great works, I pray thee, mightful God, to draw me after thee unto the sweet smell or thine ointments, and so make me now worthy with all reverence, with perfect meekness and holiness, with full contrition and tears of true devotion, with spiritual comfort and gladness of thy presence.

O blessed body in form of bread, come and enter into my mouth and heart, so that by thy presence my soul may be fed and fastened to thee with perfect charity !

Lord God, fulfil me with grace and strengthen me with thy might, that I may ever hereafter govern my life after thy will, and live in thee and thou in me !

Jesu, for thy great bounty save me from all perils; teach and comfort my soul in all doubts and dreads ; turn from me all vices ; suffer nothing to abide in my heart, but only thee, Lord, that art my soul's life and physician, that 1 may with

gladness find medicine and health in my soul by virtue of thy blessed presence.

Look not, Lord, on my wickedness and manifold unkindness and great negligence, but rather, gracious Lord, on thy sovereign mercy and endless goodness. For thou sayest thyself, Lord, that at what hour a sinner sorroweth for his sins, at that hour thou receivest him into thy mercy and into thy grace. Lord, this is the hour and the time that I would be very sorry, and forsake my sins, and follow thee with holy virtues: therefore now I trust thy mercy descendeth into my soul.

Also, Lord, thou sayest that if a sinner have true sorrow for his sins, thou wilt never have mind of those sins afterward. Now, gracious Lord, put all my wretched sins out of thy mind, so that they hinder not the fruit of virtues nor the influence of thy holy grace in my needy soul.

For, soothly, Lord, thou art that holy lamb without spot or stain of sin that this day and every day art offered to thine everlasting Father of heaven for the redemption of all the world, and specially for all them that apply them unto thy mercy.

O thou most sweet heavenly meat! O joy of angels ! O souls' strength ! O precious body that givest endless health ! O most pleasant

ghostly drink ! bring into mine inward mouth that holy sweet taste of thine healthful presence : kindle in me the fervour of thy charity : shed into me the plenteousness of virtues : increase in me the gifts of grace.

I beseech thee, bow thine high heaven and come down to me, so that I may be knit and united to thee, and made one spirit with thee. (That is to understand, bow thine high majesty that is of the highest heaven, and come down to me that am lowest of thy chosen souls ;—thou that art high, and I that am low.)

O thou worshipful sacrament, I beseech thee that all mine enemies be put away from me by strength of thee, and all my sins forgiven, and all my wickedness excluded by the blissful presence of thee.

And, gracious Lord, do thou give me good purpose ; my wicked ways do thou correct and amend ; and all my works and deeds do thou dispose after thy will. May my will and understanding by thee, sweet Lord, here be made clear with a new light of thy grace ; and mine affection inflamed with fire of thy holy grace and love ; and my hope comforted and strengthened with this blessed sacrament, so that my life be perfect, ever amending for the better : and at the last that

[Devotions for Communion]

I may from this wretched world, with a blessed departing with thee, come to the life everlasting.

For, merciful Lord Jesu, thus thyself thou saidst, Ego sum panis qui de caelo descendi; si quis manducaverit ex hoc pane, vivet in aeternum. —*I am the bread of life that from heaven descended : whoso eateth of this bread shall live endlessly.* Thou saidst also, Lord, My flesh is very meat, and my blood is very drink. Oh ! thou precious nourishment ! Oh ! thou noble restorative ! Oh ! thou mighty cordial in whom all delight and all sustenance of ghostly favour is privily hid and kept for clean souls!

O thou wretched soul of mine, whereto art thou seeking ? Elsewhere be creatures, but here is present the almighty Creator ; elsewhere be relics of saints, but here is present the Lord and king and maker of all saints: (they may do nothing but by the virtue of this good Lord). Other things must not be beloved and worshipped, save for his love and his praise, his glory and his honour. Here is very God's Son Jesus, that took flesh and blood by the high workings of the Holy Ghost, and born of the virgin Mary, and suffered death for me on the cross, and rose from death to life the third day, and after that ascended up to heaven, and sitteth on the Father's right side, and

[Devotions for Communion

shall come at the day of doom to judge me and all mankind. In his power is both life and death ; that made heaven and hell and all the world of nought; and that only by his mercy may save me, and by his righteousness may damn me without end.

O mightful and gracious and merciful Lord, too unworthy am I to touch the least body of the saints ; and much more it behoveth me to hold myself unworthy, and to be devout and clean, and weep with tears in mine eyes, and with my heart to tremble and quake for dread, to touch so holy a thing. For thou art my Lord Christ's very body, perfect God and perfect man : and I shall not only touch, nor shall I kiss thee, but I hope verily that I shall receive thee now into my sick soul.

O thou good Lord God, thou art all purity and cleanness and holiness ; and I am all sin, filth and wretchedness, dust and ashes and worms' food. From the earth I came, and to the earth I shall return again. Thou art Lord alone, and I am all death : and how might these two great contraries dwell together ? But, gracious Lord, this again comforteth me, that thy might and thy mercy may in a moment of time cleanse me of all filth of sin, and forgive me all offences. And it is thy

Devotions for Communion]

Lord, to be merciful to sinners : therefore, gracious Lord, as it were by right of thy holy virtues I crave and ask thy mercy and thy grace to receive thee now in the sacrament, in all cleanness and purity, to the everlasting health of my sick soul. Dear Lord, grant it me, for thy great benignity ! Amen.

Ps. Miserere met Deus. R. Domtne non secun-dum actum meum. Hymnus, Vent creator spiritus. Paternoster. Ave Maria. Credo in Deum.

[Devotions for Communion

Before the receiving of our Lord thus think or say:

ALMIGHTY God, most merciful, have mercy upon me that am wretched and unkind and sinful.

I yield me to thee, almighty Jesu, and to thy blissful mother.

Mercy ! mercy 1 mercy ! dear-worthy Jesu ! and grant mercy now !

Blessed Lord that art here present, very God and man, the same Lord that madest me and all the world of nought, and boughtest with thy precious passion, and with thy holy blood, and with thy bitter death : thou that art the same that mayest save me by greatness of thy mercy, and the same Lord that mayest damn me by righteousness of thy judgement; thou that art the same Lord that I have been untrue and unkind to, in my words and in my works and in my deeds and in my thoughts ; with all the

Devotions for Communion]

limbs and parts of my body, and with all the powers of my soul I have offended thee.

Wherefore, good Lord, with thy holy humanity that is here present, make therewith oblation and satisfaction to God thy Father for me, so that, by the virtue of thy blessed body, all the powers of my body may be made obedient, quick and ready in thy service, and be full recon ciled now to thy pleasure. And with the purity, the holiness, the fairness, the cleanness and the brightness and the sweetness and the unspeak-ableness of thy sweet soul that is here present, make therewith oblation and satisfaction to God thy Father ; for that I have defiled and defaced the three powers of my soul, so that, by the virtue of thy holy soul, this my soul may now be recon ciled again to thy likeness, and so be inhabited with virtues and endued with grace, and inflamed with thy love, and be made thy habitation and thy resting-place.

And with thine almighty Godhead that is here prescnt, (to whom nothing is impossible, but all things are possible), make oblation and satis faction to thyself for me, for that I have offended by my feebleness, by my folly, by my sin, by my lack of grace ; that now, by thy divine might, by thy divine wisdom, by thy great goodness and the

\Devotionsfor Communion

plenteousness of thy grace, I may be reconciled to thee, and full satisfaction be made for all offences and trespasses ; and now perfect peace be made betwixt thee, almighty God, and my soul; between mankind and my soul ; between my soul and myself; so that I may peaceably rest in thee and thou in me.

Jesu, grant it of thy bounty : and after this mortal life that I may endlessly live in thy pre sence, and there see thee face to face, and ever joy in thy goodness and bliss everlasting. Amen.

Devotions for Gommumon

This that followeth say or think soon after the communion :

ELCOME, my gracious creator ! Welcome, my victorious redeemer !

Welcome, my kindly saviour !

Welcome, very God, sovereign and endless wisdom, sovereign and endless God, and blessed life of all things and incomprehensible save of thyself!

Welcome, mine high pontiff!

Welcome, mine archbishop !

Welcome, mine high emperor !

Welcome, mine high rich king !

Welcome, my worthy prince!
Welcome, my noble lord!
Welcome, my sweet love!
Welcome, my dear-worthy spouse!
Welcome, my reverend lord!
Welcome, my kindly father!
Welcome, my tender nurse!

[Devotions for Communion

Welcome, my loving mother!
Welcome, my true cousin!
Welcome, homely brother!
Welcome, my helper!
Welcome, my teacher!
Welcome, my castle and my tower, and my safe refuge and my defender!
Welcome, my very God that died on the rood!
Welcome, my sweet Jesu, that for me shed-dedst thy heart-blood!
Welcome, son of the virgin Mary!
Welcome, my Lord of great mercy!
Welcome, my rightful judge when I shall die!
Welcome, thou very joy and food of angels!
Welcome, thou love and happiness of all saints!
Welcome, thou desire and comfort of all Christian souls!
Welcome, my very hope!
Welcome, my safe health!
Welcome, all my felicity, my solace, my comfort and endless wealth!
Welcome, now, my gracious Lord, for thou art the life of my soul, and thou art the Lord that I would have; thou art the love that I have

Devotions for Communion]

thus longed after; thou art the spouse that I desire to find.

Good Lord, grant me for to feel thy presence ghostly and inwardly, and array me with thy gracious virtues, and inflame me with thy holy love, and give me them ail: for then have I all that I covet, and all that I desire, and all that I need.

For thou art my very paradise and my excellent heaven above all heavens, my sovereign and endless joy, my singular joy, and my full sufficiency in thy divine majesty,—three Persons and but one God in unity and might, that made all things of nought. Thy wisdom ordained all things; thy goodness multiplieth and keepeth all things that thou mayest do with thy wisdom in heaven, in earth, in purgatory and in hell. To thee is nothing impossible, for all things are possible; for thou art all, and thou doest all that is done.

Therefore all might, all wisdom and all goodness; and all glory and all grace and all sweetness; all virtues, all victories and all honours; all bliss, all joys and all magnificence; worship thee, praise thee, glorify and magnify thee, everlasting God without end. Amen.

Ps. Nunc Dimittis (with other Latin Devotions).

[Devotions for Communion

A meditation after communion, with mental prayer and inward thinkings to God y prostrate on the ground.

OMY dear sweet Lord, how blessedful had I been sometime, if I might have received into my mouth one drop of thy precious blood running out of the precious open wounds of thy holy body. But, sweet Lord, I have not only received a drop or two of that precious liquor ; but now I have received all the whole substance of the high Godhead, the glorious excellent soul, and blessed and holy and precious body, all whole, joined to my soul and body !

Dear Lord, how worthily should the presence of thee move the inward affection of my poor heart! What may be shewed to me more of love, than thus homely to knit me to thee, whom mine heart desireth ? and thou sayest that it is thy delight to dwell with the sons of men : and them that with meekness come to thee thou wilt

Devotions Jor Communion

not cast out from thee, but thus thou receivest them into thine arms and into thine inmost heart.

Therefore now, my happy soul, be thou com forted ! for whom thou hast languored after and sought, thou hast found and received—Christ thy spouse, in very truth fully contained in this holy sacrament.

But, Lord, right as my bodily eye may not see thy humanity that is here present with me, so saint Symeon, bearing thee in his arms, might not see thy Godhead, but only with the eye of true belief, as I see thee now verily present. But, good Lord, what is bodily sight to me ? since those eyes are affirmed blessed by thee, which see not, as the scribes and pharisees, fleshly ; but, as the chosen disciples did, ghostly.

Therefore now, my soul, taste and see ! For thy Lord is sweet, soft and meek, and delectable to thee ; so that now, for wondering at his good ness, I might faint in myself inwardly, crying and saying :

Oh ! the high might and worthiness ! Oh ! the high wisdom and riches ! Oh 1 the high courtesy and gentleness ! O, my Lord God ! that so abundantly givest thyself to me in this holy sacrament, that I may say and desire with

[Devotions for Communion

the prophet that my soul in my body rejoiceth in the almighty living God ! My Saviour, mine heart is inflamed within thy love ! May mine ears be set wide apart from fleshly lusts, and set for ghostly delights of thee ! Here is my rest in the world of worlds ! Here shall I dwell ; for supremely do I choose thee.

For thou art my light and my health ; whom should I dread ? Thou art the defender of my life ; whom should I fear, but thee, Lord ? For thou hast not despised thine unworthy servant nor turned thy face from me; but of thy pure goodness hast visited me with thy glorious presence, O thou endless Trinity !

O glorious Godhead ! the which, by union of divine nature, hast made the body and the holy blood of thine only-begotten Son to be so praiseworthy that it is sufficient to ransom all mankind ; and therewith hast this day fed my needy soul, so that I have received all the whole essential being of the holy Trinity ! O thou endless God ! O thou light above all other lights, of whom cometh all lights! and fire passing all other fires ! For thou art the fire that burneth and wasteth not, but thou consumest all sin and natural love that thou findest in a soul. And yet even that thou wastest not painfully, but

Devotions for Communion]

floodest it with increasing love. Thou fillest it, yet it is not thus satisfied, but desireth ever more and more of thy lovely fire. O endless, sovereign God! who stirreth thee or moveth thine infinite goodness to illuminate me, thine unworthy creature, with the light of thy truth ? Thou thyself art the same fire and cause of love that moved thee for to shew me mercy! Thus, on whatever side I turn me, I find none other but the depth and fire of thy most flaming charity.

Oh ! thou goodness above all goodness ! Thou alone art fairness, O thou endless cleanness !

Oh 1 thou endless sweetness, and unspeakable brightness !

Oh ! thou endless lightness, with mirth and melody !

O thou art worthiest, mightiest, wisest, richest; most bounteous, most homely and courteous ; and in love and in goodness without measure!

Oh ! that I had clear sight of the blessed Trinity, beholding with undazzled eyes, strong charity ; love delectable ; love continual; meek est awefulness ; highest marvel; deepest search ing ; and most plenteous spending ; mirth without measure ; and joy and felicity without ending !

To come to this unspeakable joy, thou art my very hope ; for thou hast given thine only true Son Jesu to me sacramentally, the sweetness of my salvation.

Oh ! endless deepness ! Oh ! endless God head ! Oh ! deep sea !

What mightest thou give me more than thy self, that wastest not nor consumest in the heart of the love of a soul ? Thou art the fire that doest away all coldness ; thou art the very light above nature, and of so great abundance of perfec tion that thou makest clear the light of faith ; in which faith I see that my soul hath life. And in that light it hath received thee, that art very light. In thy wisdom thou hast given me true knowledge, and in thy mildness I have found love of thee. Whoso searcheth mine heart findeth not my virtues, but only thy charity whereby I may purify both soul and body in thy holy blood. Thou movest with the same blood, opening the gate of heaven to mankind.

O thou endless Trinity, thou art the deep sea, in the which the more I enter the more I find : thou art insatiable for a soul. He that filleth him in thy deepness is not so filled but that he alway hungereth after thee, desiring with light to see thee in endless light. For as the

hart desireth after the spring of running water, so I in my soul desire to go out of the dark prison of my body, to see thee in very truth as thou art.

O my Lord God almighty, how long time shall thy glorious face be hid from mine eyes ? O thou most excellent beauty ! O thou worthy hope and refuge ! thus reforming again my soul to thy likeness ! O thou most merciful and marvellous largeness ! O thou who art all wounded in love ! Why art thou so wounded in the love of me ? For often in my conduct I have unkindly forsaken thee and thou again seekest me ! Often in my conduct I flee from thee, and thou comest near to me ! More near mayest thou never come than to send thine only Son Christ Jesu thus lovingly into my soul, with light of truth of thy presence.

Wherefore now I thank thee, merciful Lord, with all the might and strength that thou hast given me, for all thy gifts and great benefits that thou hast done to me. And specially I give thee thanks, kindly God, that this day thou hast thus fed me with thy precious body, by the which I hope to have health of soul and everlasting life with thee, when I depart hence. Oh ! how shall I, a poor wretch, give thanks for 144

this fervent charity and love that thou hast shewed me ? For I am one that is nought 5 therefore thou alone, sweet Father art he that is. Therefore thou shalt take thanks of thine endless goodness, and art charity for me !

O Holy Ghost, come, good Lord, come and inflame mine heart with the burning beams of love, that I may with virtuous sweetness con tinually yield acceptable thanks to the glorious Trinity.

O ye three Persons and one God, glory and praise with all reverence be offered to you of afl good creatures, without end. Amen.

Ps. Benedicite omnia opera (with other Latin devotions).

Form of Devotion at Communion

Before receiving the most holy sacrament

KNOW well that all works and merits of men, be they never so holy, are unworthy for the receiving of thee, Lord, who art so worthy! so mighty! so benign! so merciful as thou art in all need!

Ah! ah! true merciful Lord! how much more then am I unworthy that sin every day, and, as a man incorrigible, dwell therein still!

Ah! good Lord, why do I such despite to thee as to cast thee, my Lord God so precious, into so foul a pit of my conscience? For soothly, my sweet and gracious sovereign Lord, I acknowledge to thee that there is no ditch more foul than my soul.

Ah! Lord, Lord, that art so humble and so meek, what shall I do with thee, kindly Lord? Why! Shall I leave thee, Lord, in that foul place? Soothly, Lord, I dare not—but that I hope in thy mercy.

But, sovereign mightful Lord, I trow that thy mercy is endless; more than all mine horrible foul and wretched sin: therefore I am all trusting in thy goodness, merciful Lord.

I venture to receive thee, sweet Lord, as a sick man receiveth a medicine. Thou art a true physician, Lord, and soothly I am sick! Therefore I take thee for to be made whole through thee. And the more sick I am, the so much more would I be made whole by thee, my sweet Lord; and the more need that I have of thee, the more intently and busily should I think to call upon thee. Therefore, Lord, in the healing of my deadly sickness there shall well be shewed and commended the greatness of thy goodness.

Devotions for Communion]

After receiving the holy sacrament.

(If communion be followed by sensible devotion^ let a man think thus:)

EE, see! every sinful creature! This doeth our merciful and gracious Lord to me, for to shew to me my wickedness, and for to overcome my wretchedness with the plenty of his goodness. See, see! Well may I be joyful, for he maketh me, a dead man, for to feel life; and me, a foul worm, for to taste heavenly delight.

Ah! ah! since our Lord is so courteous to me that alway live in sin, what trow I he would do to me, if I fully offer myself to him? In truth he would do much better than eye can see, or any heart may think....

[Devotions for Communion

(If communion be not followed by sensible devotion^ it is good that a man think that it is a token of great sickness or even of great death of sin, or else that it is permitted by God for to make him a man. But a man should ever conceive that he is continually in default against that mightful Lord, and therefore should he full meekly and lowly say to him thus:)

AH! Lord, Lord, now full merciful Lord, what shall I do?

I have put fire in my bosom, and I feel none heat of it!

Lo, lo! Lord ever full merciful to sinful wretches! I have put honey in my mouth, and I feel no manner of sweetness thereof!

Ah! good Lord Jesu Christ, have pity upon me, the most unkind and froward wretch, for I have received a sovereign medicine, and yet I feel none the more healed!

PART IV GENERAL DEVOTIONS

[General Devotions

Celuf

Credo in deum patrem omnipotentem

IN thee, God Father, I believe,
Who art First Person full of might,
That all of nought hast made to move
Both heaven and earth, both day and night,
And in thine one-begotten Son
Born of thyself before all thing, Jesus our Lord, the next Person,
And one with God in heaven being.
The one same God that aye hath been, After conceived by the Holy Ghost,
And born on earth of maiden clean Became a man in meekness most.
And right as in the Trinity
Be Persons three, but substance one,
Right so in thee be substance three, God, soul, body — and one Person.

Under Pilate thou sufPredst pain Of thy free-will, mankind to save,
Nailed on a cross and thereon slain, And taken down and laid in grave.
In soul thou went deep hell within And took thy part (it was good right),
But up thou rose in flesh and skin, On the third day by Godly might.

I

Thou rose to heaven in thy manhead ;
There sittest at thy Father's side : But over all is thy Godhead,—
There's none that him from thee may hide.
Thence shalt thou come us all to doom, Both quick and dead of Adam's seed,
With open wounds and face of gloom ;— This doctrine maketh true men dread.
I believe in the Holy Ghost,
The Third Person in Trinity; Of which Three none is more nor most,
But all one God in Persons three.
The Holy Ghost maketh holy church, Of faithful men, by communing ;

Each to other what they can work In holiness and good living.
Forgiveness I believe of sin,
By the Holy Ghost and sacrament,
If I may ghostly to it win ; Or else himself is aye present.
Though he never so present be,
Yet he desires for full meekness That I should do what is in me,
Lest pride should stay my forgiveness.
And I believe with my whole mind The Holy Ghost shall knit again
The soul to the flesh of all mankind ;
That flesh shall rise which death hath slain.
The Holy Ghost shall give also
Eternal life to all true men ; That we may here assent thereto,
I counsel we say all, amen.

General Devotions]

ATHER, Son and Holy Ghost,
Lord to thee I make my moan ; Stedfast king of might the most, Almighty God upon the throne : I pray thee, Lord, that thou make haste To pardon what I have misdone.

Father of heaven, to thee I pray Almighty Lord, that thou me lead In stable truth the rightful way At mine ending, when I shall dread ; Thy grace I ask both night and day ; Have mercy now on my misdeed ; Of mine asking say me not nay, But help me, Lord, in all my need.

Sweet Jesu, that for me was born,
Hear thou my prayer both loud and still;
[General Devotions
For pains that me are laid before Full oft I sigh and weep my fill : Full often have I been foresworn When I have wrought against thy will; Let thou me never be forlorn, Lord Jesu Christ, for my deeds ill.

Holy Ghost, I pray to thee
Night and day with good intent :
In all my sorrows comfort me,
Thy holy grace to me be sent ;
And let me never bounden be
In deadly sin, that I be shent ; Ruined
For Mary's love, that maiden free
On whom thou truly made descent.

I pray thee, Lady meek and mild That thou wilt pray for my misdeed, For the love of that same child That thou saw on the rood to bleed. Ever and aye have I been wild, My sinful soul is aye a-dread : Mercy, Lady ! thou me shield ! Help thou me aye at all my need.

Mercy, Mary, maiden fair! I/et thou me never in sin dwell ; 157
General Devotions]
Pray for me, that I beware,
And shield me from the fire of hell.
Certes, Lady, well I know
That all my foemen thou may fell ;
Therefore my grief to thee I shew,
With mournful mood my tale I tell.

Bethink thee, Lady, ever and aye, Of women all thou bears the flower ; For sinful man, as I thee say, Our Lord has done thee great honour Help me, Lady, as well thou may ; Thee behoves be my counsellor ; Of counsel, Lady, I thee pray, And also of help and of succour.

Night and day in weal and woe In all my sorrow comfort me ; And be my shield against my foe, And keep me, if thy will so be, From deadly sin that me will slay ; Mercy, Lady, fair and free ! That which is fallen take away, For thy mercy and thy pity.

At mine ending stand thou by me, When I from hence set forth and go:
I Genera I Devotion*
When I shall quake and dread-full be, And all my sins are full of woe. Since aye my hope has been in thee, I pray thee, Lady, help me there ; All for the love of that sweet tree Where Jesus spread his body bare.

Jesu, by that long agony That thou would on the rood-tree bleed, At mine ending when I shall die, Have mercy, Lord, on my misdeed ; And heal me there of my death-wound, And guard me there at all my need : When death takes me and brings to ground, Lord, then shall I thy judgement dread.

For all my sins to do penance,
Before my death, Lord, grant thou me ;
And space for very penitence,
With all my heart beseech I thee ;
Thy mercy is my confidence,
My foolishness do thou pity :
And on me take thou not vengeance,
Lord, for thy debonnairety
Lord God, as thou art full of might Whose love is sweetest for to taste ;

General Devotions]

My life amend, my deeds set right, For Mary's love, the maiden chaste : And bring me to that very light; (To look on thee is joy the most !) To look on thee !—that joyful sight ! Father, Son and Holy Ghost. Amen.

[General Devotions

8n Intercession to Jesu*

LORD God of might withouten end, I to thy hand to-day commend My soul and my body, And all my friends especially ; To quick and dead grant thou a share, Lord God, of this thy bedesman's prayer ; And keep us that on earth are here, (For the prayer of thy mother dear And all thy saints that are in heaven), From the deadly offences seven, And from snare of the evil wight, From sudden death by day or night. Shield us from the pains of hell That bitter are to bear, and fell; And with thy grace fulfill us all, That we be ready to thy call : And let us never part from thee As thou for us has died on tree ; Grant us, Lord, that so it be ! Amen, Amen, for charity !

General Devotions]

(Eummen&attons for

(i) A prayer in view of death

O GLORIOUS Jesu ! O meekest Jesu ! O most sweet Jesu ! . I pray thee that I may have true confession,

contrition and satisfaction ere I die. And that I may see and receive thy holy body,
God and man, Saviour of all mankind, Christ
Jesu without sin. And that thou wilt, my Lord God, forgive me
all my sins for thy glorious wounds and
passion. And that I may end my life in the true faith of
holy church, and in perfect love and charity
with my fellow-christians, since they are thy
creatures. And I commend my soul into thy holy hands,
through the glorious help of thy blessed
Mother of mercy, our Lady, saint Mary, and
all the holy company of heaven.

[General Devotions

The holy body of Christ Jesu be my salvation
of body and soul. Amen. The glorious blood of Christ Jesu bring my soul
and body into the everlasting bliss. Amen. I cry God mercy ! I cry God mercy ! I cry
God mercy ! Welcome my maker ! Welcome my redeemer !
Welcome my saviour ! I cry thee mercy with heart contrite for my
great wickedness that I have had to thee.

Amen.

(ii) A commendation for death; looking upon a cross or image.

LORD, Father that art in heaven, I ask thee mercy for all that I have trespassed : and may the free passion of our Lord Jesu Christ, the which he suffered for mankind, merciful Father, of thy goodness be betwixt me and mine evil deeds: And may the great merit of our Lord Jesu Christ be pleasing to thee for all that I should have merited and done, and did not: And also, merciful Lord, Father of heaven, if it be thy will, I beseech thee that all the benefits that our Lord Jesu Christ, after thy bidding did here in earth for the salvation of mankind, stand betwixt me and thy wrath.

And, blissful Lady, Mother of mercy, saint Mary, queen of heaven, lady of all this world, and empress of hell, as thou before all women didst merit, through the goodness of God, to bear, without loss of thy maidenhood, Jesu Christ, Saviour of mankind ; so do thou beseech thy blessed son for me, that all my sins be forgiven.

And, Lord almighty, Jesu Christ, since thy holy gospel witnesseth that thou wilest not the death of sinful man, but that he be turned from sin and live ; have mercy on me, a sinful wretch, after thy word ; and as thou blamedst Simon for that he had indignation that Mary Magdalen, for her sins, should approach thee ; have mercy on me most sinful: And, Lord Jesu, as thou calledst Zaccheus and Paul and divers others from their sins ; despise not me that come to thee willingly, without any such calling : and though I have lain long in my sin, think, Lord, on the great mercy that thou hadst and shewedst to man, that he should not be ashamed nor despair of thy mercy, although he had lain long in sin ; when thou hadst no disdain to raise Lazarus, although he had lain in his grave four days, corrupting.

And therefore I trust to thee, Lord, for thou art Father almighty, in whose mercy I trust, to whose refuge I flee. With great desire I come to thee in haste : Lord, despise me not, though I be wretched and sinful, for that I trust fully to thy help in all my great need. For I acknowledge that I cannot help myself nor redeem myself with my deeds ; but stedfastly I trust in thy passion, that it sufficeth to make full satisfaction to the Father of heaven for my sins.

Therefore, Lord, bring me out of care and have mercy on me. I trust not to my deeds, but I despise to trust in them ; fully trusting to thy mercy, despising my wicked deeds. For thou art my God in whom I trust stedfastly is all might and mercy and good-will, through which I hope to be saved. And therefore to thee, that art full of mercy, I acknowledge my sin the which I have done through mine own fault. I acknowledge my guilt : have mercy on me ! for I know truly that thou deniest thy mercy to none that truly trust thereto. And in trust thereof I forsake with all my heart this life, to live with thee. Into thine hands, Lord almighty and merciful, I commit my soul. For from the beginning of this world hath thy mercy been ready to sinful men, and so I trust it shall be to me in mine end.

Therefore, God my Lord, full of truth, take my soul, for it is thine ! Do thereto as it pleaseth thee ! For I wit well of thy goodness it shall fare better than it hath deserved. Receive it and keep it, for in thy merciful hands I put it. Amen.

of

THEY that withouten law do sin: withouten law shall die therein : For at that dreadful

doom truly : shall each have
that he is worthy : That day shall no man be excused : of nothing
that he here has used : The sinful shall no mercy have : and nothing
that day may them save : They shall have none for them to plead : nor
them to counsel at their need : Nor any saint for them shall pray : this may be
called a dreadful day ! The day of great deliverance : the day of wreak
and of vengeance : The day of wrath and wretchedness : the day of
bale and bitterness : The day of 'plaint and accusing : the day of
answer and hard reckoning : The day of dread and of trembling : the day of
weeping and of groaning :

General Devofions]

The day of crying and loud sorrow : the day of
everlasting woe : The day of flying and great affray : the day of
parting from God for aye.

Mortis vel vitae brevis est vox — he ; Vemte ; Aspera vox lie; vox est jucunda Venite. Deo gratias. Jhtsus. Maria. Johannes. Passio domlnl nostri Jesu Christi, &c. Humilitas. Charitas. Qbedieniia. Labor. [The word of life or death is short — Go ; Come. Bitter is the word Go ; sweet is the word Come ;

Thanh to God. Jesus. Mary. John. The passion of our Lrrd Jesus Christ, &c.
Humility. Love. Obedience. Labour.

[Genera Devotions

Epigram

TUT EAVEN is won with woe and shame ;
Hell is won with glee and game : I ask thee then, which of these two On earth were better,- -weal or woe ?

General Devotions]

(i) To the Blessed Trinity.

LMIGHTY God in Trinity -IL From all my heart be thanks to thee For thy good deed, that thou me wrought, And with thy precious blood me bought, And for all good thou lends to me, O Lord God, blessed may thou be ! All honour, joy and all loving Be to thy name without ending. Amen.

(ii) To Jesus.

LORD Jesu Christ, God almighty, With all my heart be thanks to thee, That me man shaped and made of nought, And of vile matter me forth-brought, My body of matter fashioned, In joints together thou has knitted ; My soul thou made through breath of thine, 170

[Genera Devotions

And gave me limbs all fair and fine ; From a mirk dungeon brought me right, (That is my mother's womb,) to light; And then begat me thy child new-born, Through baptism, that was the fiend's child
lorn.

Five senses of body thou gave to me, And skill wherewith they ruled be. And though I have wrought against thy law, Thy good thou will not from me draw j A traitor false against thee aye, Who sins against thee every day. Thou sends me here through providence Each day my needful sustenance, That is to say meat and clothes free And all that needful is to me. Thou has borne with me, and 'venged thee not Of all my sin against thee wrought; And yet thou bears, and gives me space To turn to thee and take thy grace ; Aye, when in the fiend's power I fall From final loss does me recall, Which I for sinning was worthy ; But thou has covered me with mercy ; And aye has spared me, and yet spares ; And keeps me from the devil's snares, Against his darts has been my shield ;

And has saved me in youth and eld, From many perils in many states, And from mischance and sudden deaths. For all that here rehearsed is, And for all goods and kindnesses, That thou to me, a sinful caitiff, Has graciously done in this my life, I thank thee, Lord, with all loving ; And pray thou take me in thy keeping, Henceforth as ever, save me again, And grant thy grace while I remain To mend my life and live in all cleanness, That I may dwell with thee in bliss endless.

Amen.

[Genera Devotions

fi $ragn of te Jpibe fop of out l,abg, in !); any of tie jptbe gorrofos

LA.DY, for thy joys five Teach me the way of righteous life.

Amen.

Now meekest and joyfullest Lady, saint Mary, for the joy that thou had when thou conceived thy dear son of the Holy Ghost in the greeting of the angel — the which joy was so great that if the angel had abode longer than to make his message, thine heart had cloven for great joy and love in God, and thou had died, if thou had not been strengthened of the Holy Ghost   now, Lady, for that great joy, have mercy on me, a sinful wretch. Paternoster. Ave Maria.

Sweetest and joyfullest Lady, for the great joy that thou had in the birth of thy sweet son Jesu ; have mercy on me, a sinful wretch : for as thou conceived him of the Holy Ghost with great joy and without any sin, so thou bare him

with great joy and without any sorrow. Amen. Paternoster.

As the sun shines through the glass and lightens the place within, and the glass is not broken nor stained of the sun when he shines, nor when he withdraws his beams, nor after, but is aye clear and whole: right so, Lady, when the Godhead shone in thy soul and took manhood of thee and was born of thee, thou was not stained; but thou was hallowed of his presence, so that thou might never be stained. Paternoster. Ave Maria.

Now blissfullest and joyfullest Lady, for the honour of the glorious passion that thy blessed son suffered for us sinful wretches ; have mercy on me, a sinful wretch, for the bloody wounds that he suffered, and the precious blood that he shed for us on the glorious cross that he was nailed on for us, and the shameful death, and all the bitter pains that he suffered ; and for all the sorrows that thou had for his pains.

Now, dear Lady, for the perturbance that thou had when Symeon said to thee, The sword of sorrow, he said, shall pass through thine own soul; —pray thy dear son to help me and to deliver me out of all my sins, and to keep me from a.11 ill. Amen. Paternoster. Ave Maria,

Dear Lady, for the sorrow thou had when thy son was lost from thee three days, and thou sought him with weeping heart; pray thy son to give me contrition of all my sins in the end of my life. Amen. Paternoster. Ave Maria.

Dear Lady, for the sorrow that thou had when thou wist in spirit that thy son was taken and should suffer death ; pray thy son to deliver me out of all tribulation of body and of soul. Paternoster. Ave Maria.

Now, dear Lady, for the sorrow that thou had when that thou saw thy dear son hang on the cross, with fresh wounds new-made, red with his own blood ; pray thy blessed son to make me burning in his love so that I never forget him. Paternoster.

Dear Lady, for the sorrow that thou had when that thy dear son lay dead in thine arms ; pray thy son to save me from damnation and from hard pains when that I shall pass out of this life, and from the great dread and the temptations or fiends, and from all mischiefs both bodily and ghostly, and grant me his endless bliss. Amen. Paternoster. Ave.

Dear Lady, for the great joy that thou had in his glorious resurrection, when thou saw him risen from death to life, and IIQW restoration of '75

General Devotions']

angels and redemption of mankind was made by his passion ; have mercy on me, a sinful wretch. Paternoster. Ave Maria.

Now, dear and loveliest Lady, for the great joy that thou had when that thou saw thy sweet son Jesus ascend into heaven from whence he came, in the manhood that he took of thee, for to be king of heaven, lord of earth, emperor of hell, King of all kings, Lord of all lords, to ordain thee a mansion above all holy angels and all saints, next to the holy Trinity, and for to udge both dead and quick at his will; have mercy on me, a sinful wretch. Paternoster. Ave Maria.

Joyfullest and graciousest Lady, for that great joy that thou had when thy blessed son Jesu Christ, almighty God in Trinity, crowned thee queen of heaven, lady of earth, empress of hell, lady and queen of all holy angels and all saints, Mother of mercy, succour and comfort to the salvation of all mankind ; have mercy on me, a sinful wretch ; and on all those that I am bound to pray for ; and on all those that trust in my prayers ; and on all those that holy church prays for, quick and dead. Amen. Paternoster. Ave Maria.

General Devotions

Jfeong to

HAIL be thou, Mary, the mother of Christ, Hail, thou most blessed that ever bare child !

Hail, that conceivedst of thy free-will The Son of God, both meek and mild I Hail, maid sweet that ne'er was defiled ! Hail, well and wit of all wisdom ! Hail, thou flower ! hail, fairest in field ! Ave regma caelorum !

Hail, comely queen, comfort of care ! Hail, blessed Lady both fair and bright 1 Hail, the salvour of every sore ! Hail, the lamp of gleaming light! Hail, blessed maid in whom Christ was pight ! * Hail, joy of man both all and some ! * Placed. Hail, pinnacle in heaven and height ! Mater regis angdorum*

General Devotions]

Hail, thou fairest that ever God found, Who choosed thee to his own bower ! Hail, the lantern that aye is lightened ! To thee should bow both rich and poor. Hail, spice sweetest of all savour ! Hail, of whom all joy has come ! Hail, of all women the fruit and flower, Velut rosa vel /ilium /

Hail, be thou goodly ground of grace ! Hail, blessed star upon the sea I Hail, thou of comfort in every case I Hail, the chiefest in charity ! Hail, well of wit and of mercy ! Hail, that bare Jesus, God's own Son ! Hail, tabernacle of the Trinity I Funde preces ad filium /

Hail, be thou virgin of virgins ! Hail, blessed Mother ! hail, blessed May Hail, thou nurse of sweet Jesus ! Hail, chiefest in chastity, sooth to say ! Lady, so keep us in our last day That we may come to thy kingdom ! For me and every Christian pray, Pro salute fidetium. Amen.

[General Devotions

to a Guartnau

AH! good courteous angel, ordained to my •* ^ guidance, I know well my feebleness and my folly. Also I wot well that strength have I none to do God's service, but only of his gift and of your busy keeping. The wisdom that I have cometh not of me, but of what God will send me by your good enticing.

Now, good gracious angel, I ask your lowly mercy, for little heed have I taken of your good busy-ness: but now I thank you, as well as I can; with full heart beseeching you that you keep me truly this day and evermore, sleeping and waking, with safe defending and your holy teaching. Defend me and keep me from bodily harms, defend me and keep me from ghostly perils, to God's worship and the saving of my soul. Teach me and instruct me to use my senses most for God's worship and pleasure.) Feed me with devotion and savour of ghostly sweetness. Comfort me, when there is need, against my ghostly enemies; and suffer me not to lose that grace that is granted me: but, of your worthy office, keep me in God's service to my life's end. And after the passing from the body present my soul unto the merciful God. For, though I fall all day by mine own frailty, I take you to witness that ever I hope in mercy. Gladly would I worship thee: and I would, to your liking therefore, worship God for you; and you also in him, after his holy teaching. I thank him with this holy prayer. Pater noster. Deo gratias.

[General Devotions

rawi to tfte

SWEET angel, to me so dear,
That night and day standeth me near,
Full lovingly with mildest mood:
Offer for me, to Jesu our king,
Thanking, loving, love, praising,
For his gifts all great and good;
As thou goest 'twixt him and me,
And know'st my life in each degree,
Saying it in his presence.
Ask me grace to love him truly,
To serve my Lord with full heart duly,
With my daily diligence.
Keep me from vice and every peril,
While thou with me dost daily travel;
In this world of wickedness
Set me my petitions granted,
By thy prayers daily haunted,—
If it please thy holiness.

Collect of tfee &nael ffiuartitan

The

SWEET angel that keepest me, Bring me to bliss I pray to thee.

The Collect.

MY Lord Jesu Christ, as it hath pleased thee to assign an angel to wait on me, daily and nightly, with great attention and diligence: so, I beseech thee, through his going betwixt us that thou cleanse me from vices, clothe me with virtues, grant me love and grace to come, see and have without end thy bliss before thy fair face : that livest and reignest, after thy glorious passion, with the Father of heaven and with the Holy Ghost, one God and Persons three, without end in bliss. Amen.

SHe bbep of amt Spirit, rtjat fs in a Dilate tijat is ealleij Conscience

AH ! dear brethren and sisters, I see that many would be in religion that may not, either for poverty, or for dread of their kin, or for bond of marriage ; and therefore I make here a book of the religion of the heart, that is of the abbey of the Holy Ghost, that all those that may not be in religion bodily, may be so in ghostly manner.

Ah ! Jesu, mercy! Where may this abbey best be founded, and this religion ? Now, certes, nowhere so well as in a place that is called Con science; and whoso will, let him be busy to found this holy religion; and that may every good Christian man and woman do, that will be busy thereabout.

AND at the beginning, it is seemly that the place of this conscience be cleansed clean of sin ; to the which cleansing the Holy Ghost shall send two maidens that are wise ; the one is called Righteousness^ and the other is called Love-of-C'leanness : these two shall cast from the con science and heart all manner of filth of foul thoughts and desires.

When the place of the conscience is well cleansed, then shall the foundation be made, large and deep, and this two maidens shall make ; the one is called Meekness^ that shall make the foun dation deep through lowliness of herself: the other is called Poverty, that makes it large and wide above ; that casts out on each side the earth, that is to say, all earthly lusts and worldly thoughts far from the heart, so that if they hold earthly goods with love, they forget them for the time and cast no love to them, and for that time have not and set not their hearts at all on them—and these are called poor in spirit y of whom God speaks in the gospel and says that theirs is the kingdom of heaven by these words, Beati pauperes spiritu^ quoniam ipsorum est regnum caelorum. Blessed, then, is that religion that is founded in poverty and in meekness. This is the contrary of many religious that are covetous and proud.

This abbey also shall be set on a good river, that shall be the River of Tears; for such abbeys as are set on such good rivers, they are well at ease, and the more delicious dwelling is there, On such a river was Mary Magdalen founded, therefore grace and riches come all at her will. And therefore said David thus: Fluminls im petus laetificat civitatem; that is to say, the good river makei glad this city; for it is clean, safe, and rich in all good merchandise. And so the river of tears cleanses God's city—that is man's soul that is God's city ; and also the holy man says it brings out of the filth of sin the riches of virtues and of all g)od habits.

And when this foundation is made, then shaL come a damsel Buxomness on the one side, and damsel Mhericorde on the other side, for to raise the walls one storey, and to make them stalwart ; with a free heart largely giving to the poor and to them that have need : for when we do any good works of charity through the grace of God, as often as we do them in the love and the loving to of God and in good intent, so many good stones we lay in our mansion in the bliss of heaven, joined together by the love of God and of our fellow-christians. We read that Solomon made his house of great precious stones : the precious stones are alms-deeds and works of mercy and holy works, that shall be bound together with mortar of love and stedfast belief; and there-fore says David, Omnia opera eius in fide; that is to say, all his works be done in stedfast belief. And as a wall may not last without cement or mortar, so no works that we work are worth anything to God nor speedful to our souls, except they be done in the love of God and in true belief; for all that the sinful does—all is lost !

Then damsel Sufferance and damsel Fortitude shall raise the pillars, and underset them so strongly that no wind of words, anger nor strife, fleshly nor ghostly, sour nor sweet, may cast them down.

Ah ! dear brethren and sisters, whichever of you will hold this ghostly religion, and be in rest of soul and in sweetness of heart, hold thee within the cloister, and so bar thou the gates, and so carefully keep thou the wards of thy cloister, that no other temptations nor evil stir rings have entrance to thee and make thee to break thy silence, or stir thee to sin :

Fix thine eyes from foul sights, thine ears from foul hearing, thy mouth from foul speech, and thine heart from foul thoughts.

Shrift shall make thy chapter ;
Preaching shall make thy frater ;
Orison shall make thy chapel;
Contemplation shall make thy dorter, that shall be raised one storey with high yearning, and with love-quickening to God, and that shall be as far away out of worldly noise and of worldly angers and business, as thou may be for the time, through grace, for the time of prayer.

(Contemplation is a devout rising of heart, with burning love to God to do well ; and in his delights rejoices his soul, and receives somewhat of that sweetness that God's chosen children shall have in heaven.)

Ruefulness shall make the infirmary ;
Devotion shall make the cellar ;
Meditation shall make the granary ;

And when all the houses be made, then behoves it the Holy Ghost to ordain the convent of grace and of virtue ; and then shall the Holy Ghost, of whom this religion is, be the Warden and Visitor. The which God the Father founded through his power ; for thus says David, Fundavit earn a/tissimus t and that is to say, the high God the Father founded this religion , the Son through his wisdom then ordained it, as saint Paul witnesses, £>ut£ sunt a Deo ordinata sunt ; that is to say, All that is of God, the Son rules and ordains it ,• the Holy Ghost cares for it and visits it, and that we say in holy church when we say this, Veni creator spiritus, with, §>ui paracletus diccr is ; that is to say, Come thou God the Holy Ghost, and visit thou thine own, and fulfill them with grace.

And then the good Lady Charity, since she is most worthy before all others, shall be Abbess of this blessed abbey. And since as they that are in religion shall do nothing, nor say nothing, nor go no whither, nor take no gift, without leave of the Abbess, so, spiritually, shall none of such things be done without leave of Charity; for thus commands saint Paul : Omnia vestra in caritate fiant ; that is, JFhatso ye do or say or think with your heart, ye must do all in charity.

Ah ! dear brethren and sisters, what a hard commandment is here ! But it is useful for our souls that our thoughts and our words and our works be only done for love. Well-a-way, if I durst say ! for many are in religion, yet but few religious have done the commandment of saint Paul, or the counsel of the good Lady Charity that is abbess of this blessed religion ; and therefore they lose much time, and lose their reward and also their pains, greatly,—unless they amend them. Wherefore, dear brethren and sisters, be evermore awake and aware, and in all your works think deeply that whatso ye do, be it done in the love of God, and for the love of God.

[General Devotions

The Lady Wisdom shall be Prioress, for she is worthy, Nam prior omnium creaturarum est sapientia ; that is, first of all is wisdom made : and through the love and the counsel of this Prioress shall we do all that we do, and this says David : Omnia in sapientia fecisti ; that is to say, All that thou hast made thou hast made wisely,

The good Lady Meekness that at all times alike makes herself lowly and under all other, shall be Sub-prioress ; her shall ye honour and worship with buxomness.

Ah ! Jesu ! blessed is that abbey and happy is that religion that has so holy an Abbess as Charity, a Prioress as Wisdom, a Sub-prioress as Meekness!

Ah! dear brethren and sisters, blessed and happy are they !—that is to say, those souls are happy that hold the commandment of the Abbess Lady Charity, and the teaching of the Prioress Lady Wisdom, and the counsel of the Sub-prioress Lady Meekness. For whoso are buxom to these three Ladies, and rule their lives after their teaching, the Father, the Son and the Holy Ghnst shall comfort them with many ghostly joys, and help and succour them in all tempta tions and angers, that they be not overcome: 189

General Devotions]

they dread no deceits nor wiles of the fiend, for why ?—God is with them and stands aye by them as a true keeper and a strong ; and there fore says David thus : Dominus protector vitae meae ; a quo trepidabo ? as if he said, God is my champion, stalwart and true, that for me, that is 10 weak and so unmightful, has undertaken for to fight against mine enemy; whom then do I dread? now truly, right none. We read in a book of Daniel that a mightful king there was, that men called Nebuchadnezzar, that set in his realm three men that should do and ordain and settle, as governours, all the realm, so that the king should hear no noise and no complaint, but that he might be in peace and in joy and in rest in his realm. And right so the realm of the soul that these governours are in, and the religion that these three prelates are in, that is, Charity, Wisdom, and Meekness, there is peace, rest and joy in soul, and comfort in life.

Damsel Discretion, that is witty and aware, shall be Treasurer ; she shall have all in her keeping, and zealously look that all go well.

Orison shall be Chantress, that with hearty
prayers shall travail day and night. And what
Orison is, the holy man says : Oratio est Deo
sacrificium, angelis solatium, diabolo tormentum

[Genera! Devotions

that is to say, Orison is a lovely sacrifice to God, solace and joy to angels, and torment to the fiend. It witnesses in the life of saint Bartholomew that it is torment to the fiend, for the fiend cried to him and said, Bartholomese, incendunt me orationes tuae; that is to say, Bartholomew, thy prayers burn me. And that it is joy to angels, saint Austin witnesses it and says, When we pray with devotion of heart, the angels stand before us, dancing and playing, and bear our prayers up and present them to the Father of heaven; the which prayers our Lord commands to write in the book of life. Further, it is a sacrifice to God, yes, and one of those that please him most, and therefore he asks it of us where he says thus: Sacrificium laudis honorificabis me ; that is to say, Te shall worship me with sacrifice of lauding.

Jubilation, her fellow, shall help. And what 'Jubilation is, a saint tells it and says that Jubila tion is a great joy that is conceived in tears through burning love of spirit, that may not be altogether shewed nor altogether hidden. As it falls some time to those that God heartily loves that, after that they have been in prayer and orison, they are so light and so joyous in God, that whereso they go their heart sings morning songs of love-longing to their love, whom they yearn to

[General Devotions]

fold seemlily with arms of love, and sweetly to kiss with spiritual mourning over his goodness; —and yet, meanwhile, so deeply that they lack words; for love-longing ravishes their hearts so far forth that sometime they wot not what they do.

Devotion is Cellaress, that keeps the wines, both the white and the red, with deep thinking on the goodness of God, and on the pains and the anguish that he bore, and on the joys and the delights of paradise that he has ordained for his chosen.

Penance shall be Kitchener, that with great busy-ness travails day and night for to please all, and oft toils with bitter tears, for anger over her sins. She makes good meats, that is, many bitter sorrows all for her guiltinesses, and these meats feed the soul; but she spares herself through abstinence and eats but little, for do she never so much nor so manifold good works, ever seems she to herself unworthy and sinful.

Temperance serves in the frater, and she so looks to each one that moderation be over all, that none eat nor drink over-much nor over-little.

Soberness reads at the table the lives of the holy fathers, and sings and rehearses what life they

[Genera Devotions

led, for to take good ensample to do as they did, and thereby the like reward to win as they now have.

Pity is Dispenser that does service to do good to all that she may. And Mercy her sister shall be Almoner, that gives to all and can keep nought for herself.

The Lady Dread is Porter, that keeps busily the cloister of the heart and of the conscience, that chases out all wickednesses, and calls in all good virtues, and so bars the gates of the cloister and the windows, that no evil have entrance to the heart through the gates of the mouth, nor through the windows of the eyes nor of the ears.

Honesty is the Mistress of the Novices, and teaches them all courtesy, how they shall speak and go and sit and stand, and how they shall bear them without and within, how to God, how to man ; so that all that see them may take ensample of them for all goodness and all good habits.

Damsel Courtesy shall be Hostler, and them that come and abide she shall receive handily, so that each one may speak good of her. And for that neither shall be alone among the guests— (for it might fall that Dame Courtesy should be over-bold and over-hardy)—therefore shall she

General Devotions]

have a fellow-damsel Simpleness, for they two allied together through fellowship are safe and seeming ; for the one without the other is little worth meanwhile : for over-great Simpleness may make of the simple a fool or one over-nice, and over-great Courtesy may be some while either too light in cheer, or too glad or overbold for to please the guests ; but fair and well and without finding of blame may they do their office both together.

Damsel Reason shall be Purveyor, for she shall ordain within and without so skilfully that there be no default.

Damsel Faithfulness shall be Infirmaress, that shall travail about and busily serve the sick. And therefore, seeing that in the infirmary of this religion are more sick than whole, more feeble than well, and it is over-great travail to serve them all by herself, therefore she shall have a fellow-damsel Largesse, that shall see full well to each one after their needs.

A damsel prudent and wise that is called Meditation is Garnerer ; she shall gather and assemble good wheat and other good corn together, and that fully, with great plenty, through the which all the good ladies of the bouse may have their sustenance, Meditation 194

[General Devotions

is in good thoughts ot God, and of his works and of his words, and ot his creatures, and of his pains that he suffered, and of his great love that he had and has to them for whom he suffered. This garnerer had the good king David, therefore was he aye rich and in plenty ; and therefore he says in the psalter : In omnibus operibus tuis meditabar . . . die ac node; that is to say, Lord, in thy law I think night and day. This is the beginning of all perfection when man sets and fixes his heart in deep thinking on God and on his works, for often a good thought in holy meditation is better than many words said in prayer, for the holy thoughts in meditation cry in God's ears. Oft it falls that the heart is so overtaken and so ravished in holy meditation that it wots not what it does, hears, nor says, nor sees ; so deeply is the heart fastened in God and in his works that words are lacking to a man : and the stiller that he is in such like meditation the louder he cries in God's ears ; and therefore says David thus : £htf>niam tacui, dum clamarern tota die, as if he said, Lord, lo ! here, the while mine heart was in deep thoughts in thee and of thy works, it cried on thee in holy meditations, and was still, as being dumb. And thereto says the gloss, the great cries that we cry to God ire then our '95

General Devotions]

great desires and our great yearnings. And this says saint Denis, that says. When the heart is lifted and ravished to the love of God with jealous yearnings, it may not be uttered with word what the heart thinks.

This holy Meditation that is the Garnerer keeps year by year the wheat that is red without and white within, that has the side cloven, of the which men make good bread : that is called Jesu Christ, that without was red of his own blood, and white within through his own meek ness and cleanness of life, and has his side cloven with a spear ; this is that bread that we receive and eat in the sacrament of the altar. And wit thou well that the granary shall be above the cellar : also shall be meditation before devotion ; and therefore Meditation shall be Garnerer, Devotion Cellarer, and Pity Penitentiary. Of these three says the prophet David : exf fructu frumenty vini et olei sui multiplicati sunt; that is to say, Of the fruit of the wheat and wine and oil they are fulfilled. In the old law in many places God takes to his chosen these three: Serve me, he says, well, and I shall give you plenty of wheat and wine and oil. Plenty of wheat, is heartily to think on the cross and ever to have the passion of Jesu Christ heartily

General Devotions

in mind : this is meditation. Plenty of wine ? that is the well of tears, well for to weep : this is devotion. Plenty of oil, that is for to have delight and savour in God: and this is comfort. For the oil gives odour to meats, and gives light in the church and burns in the lamp; also when God's servants have deeply thought with clear heart on God and on his works, with love-longing to them, then has God pity on them, and sends them pittance of comfort and of ghostly joy. And this gives them at the beginning meditation, and this is the wheat that God promises us; then sends God afterwards the wine, that is plenty of tears and devotion that men conceive in meditation ; and, after the wine of s^veet tears, then sends he the oil of consolation that gives them savour and lightness as their acknowledgment ; and shews to them of his heavenly secrets that are hid from them that follow fleshly desires and give themselves all to the wisdom of the world and his fantasy ; and so inflames them with the bliss of his love that they taste and feel somewhat of how sweet he is, how good he is, how loving he is—but not all fully. I wot well that none may feel it fully, but his heart should burst for pleasure of joy. Saint Austin tells of a priest that, when he heard 197

General Devotions^

anything of God in which was happiness, he would be so ravished in joy that he would fall down and lie as if he were dead; and also if in that time men laid burning fire to his naked flesh, he felt it no more than does a dead corpse. Saint Bernard speaks of the words of Job that he says : Abscondit lucem in mam bus ; that is to say, God has light hid in his hands. Thou wot wel^ he that has a candle alight between his hands, he may hide it and shew it at his own will. So does our Lord to his chosen. When he will, he opens his hands and lightens them with heavenly gladness ; and when he will he closes his hands and withdraws the joy and the comfort from them. He will not that they always feel it fully, but here he gives them to taste and savour somewhat of how sweet he is, how good he is, as David says : Gustate et videte quoniam suavis est dominus ; as if God said to us, Be this comfort and this joy, that thou this short time has of me, that thou may taste and feel how sweet, how good, I am to my chosen in my bliss of the world without end: and thus he does for to draw us from worldly business and the pleasure thereof, and for to inflame our hearts with love-yearnings, for to win and to have the pleasure of that joy all at the full, to be with him in body and soul evermore without end. 198

[General Devotions

A damsel wise and well-taught that men call Jealousy, that is aye awake and busy, ever the same, to do well, shall keep the clock and shall waken the other ladies and make them early to rise and go the more willingly to their service. There are clocks in town that waken men to rise to bodily travail,—and that is the cock : and there are clocks in the city that waken the merchants to wend about their merchandise,—and that is the watchman. (And there are clocks in religion, of contemplation.) And this is the watchman of this holy religion that is founded of the Holy Ghost, namely, Jealousy^ and this is savour of perfection. And oft it falls in religion, before that the clock strikes or any bell rings, God's ghostly servants are wakened long before, and have wept before God and have washed them with their tears, and their spirit hath clothed itself with devout prayers and ghostly comfort. And why rose they so early and so timely ? Truly, for that the clock of love and damsel Jealousy had wakened them before the time that the hand-made clock struck. Ah ! dear brethren and sisters, happy are those souls that the love of God and longing towards him awakens, and that slumber not nor sleep at all in sloth of fleshly lusts! Therefore he says in the Canticle : Ego 199

General Devotions]

dormio et cor meum vigilat; that is to say, When I sleep bodily for to ease and rest my flesh, my heart is aye awake in jealousy and love-yearning to God. That soul that thus wakes to God may think with whole conscience what worldly men think, and that is this ; Jeo ay le quer a-loche, rauayle par amours ; that is to say, My heart has started from me^ wakened with love. What is this that makes the heart to wake from the flesh, and for to be, as it were, strange to him

? Truly, jealousy with love-tears and mourning, with love-longing conceived in devout uprising of heart.

When this abbey was all well ordained and God's will served, in rest and in joy and in peace of soul, then came a tyrant of the land, through his power, and placed in this holy abbey four daughters that he had, that were loathely and of evil manners, for the fiend was father of these daughters.

The first of this foul litter was named Envy^ the second Pride y the third Grudging, the fourth Fa he -judging-of-oth er.

These four daughters then has the tyrant, the devil of hell, for evil will and malice placed in this holy abbey, and they with foul uncleanness 20O

[General Devotions

have grieved and harmed the convent, so that they may have no rest nor peace, night nor day, nor joy in soul. And when the good Lady Charity^ that was Abbess, saw this, and the Lady Wisdom that was Prioress, and the Lady Meek ness Subprioress, and the other good ladies of this holy abbey, that the abbey was at the point of becoming worthless through the wickedness of the four, then they rang the chapter-bell and gathered them all together, and asked counsel what was best to do. And then Lady Discretion counselled them that they should all fall to prayer to the Holy Ghost, that is Visitor of this abbey, that he haste him for to come, as they had great need of him, for to help and visit them with his grace. And they all at her counsel, with great devotion of heart, sang unto him with a sweet stave : Fern creator spiritus. And so soon the Holy Ghost came at their desiring, and comforted them with his grace, and chased out the foul creatures, those loathely fiend's daughters, and cleansed the abbey of all the filth, and ordained it and restored it better than it was before.

Now I pray you all in charity of God that all they that read or hear of this religion be buxom with all their might, and suffer that the good 201

General Devotions]

ladies before-namtd do their office each day, spiritually, within their hearts; and let each one look wisely that he do no trespass against the rule nor the obedience of this religion and of those rulers. And if through mishap it fall that any of these four fiend's daughters seek on any wise for to have any entrance for to dwell within your hearts, or have won entrance and do dwell with you, do after the counsel of the Lady Discretion and give you to devotion with hearty prayers, in hope of God's help and of his succour, and ye shall be delivered thereof through the mercy of our Lord Jesus Christ—blessed may he be without end. Amen.

NOTES

[Notes

An Introduction to Mental Prayer.

This extract is taken from Wynkyn de Worde's edition of R. Rolle's works, 1506 ; published in the " Library of Early English Writers." It is of interest as giving, no doubt, Richard's own method of prayer.

I. i. A Song of the Love of Jesus.

These verses are extracts from a poem published in the " Library of Early English Writers." It is con tained in MS. Thornton. Possibly the author is R. Rolle.

Stanza 5, in the original, begins as follows: " My brother and syster he es by skyll, For he saide & lerede that lare That wha sa dide his fadyr will, Systers and brether till hym thay ware " > Stanza 14, in the original, is as follows : " A Jhesu, for the swetnes that in the es, Hate mynde of me when I sail wende ; With stedfaste trouthe my wittes wysse, 205

Notes]
And defende me fra the fende ;
For thy mercy forgyffe me my myssc,
That wikkede werkes my saule ne schende ;
Bot brynge me, lorde, vnto thy blysse,
With the to wonne with-owtene Ende. Amen,"

I. 2. Richard de CastrSs Prayer to Jesus. From " Hymns to the Virgin & Christ" : pub. by " Early English Text Society." Lambeth MS. No. 853, date about 1430 A.D. It is just possible that R. de Castre is the same as R. de Cirencester, a Benedictine monk and historian (d. 1401), but he is nure likely to have been a hermit like R. de Rolle. One stanza, the izth, is omitted. It runs : " Jhesu, that art with-outen lees

Almyghti god in trynyte, Ceesse these werris, & sende us pees With lastinge loue & charitee."

I. 3. The Virtues of the Name Jesus.

The short introduction to the Meditation is from Lambeth MS. No. 853. The Meditation itself, consisting of extracts from the original, is mainly from the MS. Thornton, published in the "Library of Early English Writers." It is a translation from the Latin, attributed to R. Rolle.

I. 4. The Love of Jems.

From Lambeth MS. 853. The original is a long 306

[Notes

poem of 35 stanzas. The authorship is unknown. It is published by the " Early English Text Society."

V. I. 2.

I. 5. A Loving Song to yes us. From the MS. Thornton ; by Richard Rolle. One stanza, the i6th, is omitted. It runs as follows : " Jhesu that all have made of noghte Jhesu that boghte me dere Jhesu, Joyne thi lyfe in my thoghte Swa that thay neuer bc sere."

I. 6. The Comfort of Christ Jesus.

From Lambeth MS. 853. Authorship unknown.

Stanza iii. 1. 11. " For hir loue that this councel knewe "— i.e. for the love of Mary who understood the plan of redemption.

I. 7. Short Songs to Jesus.

(1) (3) (4) These short poems by Richard Rolle are from MS. Cambr. Dd. V. 64, fol. 134-142, published in the "Library of Early English Writers."

(2) (5) MS. Thornton. Both are attributed to R. Rolle.

(6) From Royal MS. 17 B. xvii. published in " The Lay-Folks Mass-Book " by Canon Simmons. These verses were to be said at the time of the Sanctus.

(7) From the same sources as the preceding lines. To be said at the time of the reading of the Gospel,

Notes]

I. (8) (a) From the " Processional of the Nuns ot Chester," edited by Dr. Wickham Legg, for the Henry Bradshaw Society.

(b) From the York Hours, fol. clx. b. Published by Canon Simmons in " The Lay-Folks Mass-Book."

II. I. An Introduction to the Passion.

This, by R. Rolle, is from MS. Rawl. C. 285, published in the " Library of Early English Writers."

The following Meditation of R. Rolle is published in the same volume from MS. Cambr. li. I. 8, fol. 201. There are a few omissions made of passages which might check the devotion of modern Christians on account of their extreme realism.

P. 70, 11. 19, 20. This is, of course, true, since the Divine Presence is everywhere ; but to avoid con fusion it might have been better said, " Then was thou in thy soul full swiftly in hell."

The date of Richard's death is generally given as 1349 A.D., instead of 1348, as here.

II. 2. A Song to Jesus and Mary, in the Passion.

Chiefly from MS. Version : printed in the " Library of Early English Writers." Only extracts are given here ; the poem itself contains between four and five hundred lines. As it stands in the original it is the result of bringing together a great many materials. At first two hymns were combined, then the story of the Passion was added, and finally other verses addressed to 208

[Notes

our Lady. Probably the additions were made by R. Rolle. Parts of the poem appear in other MSS.

II. 3. A Meditation of the Five Wound* of Jesu Christ.

This Meditation, wrongly attributed to R. Rolle, is of unknown authorship. It is taken from MS. Univ. Coll. 87, p. 262, printed in the " Library of Early English Writers."

II. 4. A Devotion on the Symbols of the Passion.

These Devotions are from Royal MS. 17, A. 27, edited by the " Early English Text Society." Each "symbol" is represented in drawing at the head o the verses celebrating it. Other MSS., edited in the same volume, also contain the verses. A few are omitted towards the end, for devotional reasons.

II. 5. The Example of the Passion. This poem is from the Lambeth MS. 853, edited "by the " Early English Text Society."

II. 6. Meditation on the Passion and Three Arrows of Doomsday.

This Meditation, certainly by R. Rolle, is from MS. Arundel 507, fol. 48, printed in the " Library of the Early English Writers." A few lines are omitted here and there on account of their realism, which would probably interrupt the devotions of modern readers.

Notes]

The quotation from Deut. xxxii. 23 at the be ginning of the section on the Three Arrows should run : " Congregabo super eos mala et sagztfas meas " (for " tret ") " complebo in eis " = " I will heap mischiefs upon them ; I will spend mine arrows upon them " (A.V.).

The last sentence in the Meditation runs as follows In the original :

" Thus mani woundes suffird god for man kynde : ffyue thousa(nd) and fourehundreth and sexti and fiftene.

" And if thou sai ilk dai of the (y)ere fiftene : thou sal sai als many pater nostres in the hale yere."

I have not an idea what this number of the wounds signifies.

II. 7. Cant us Christi.

(i) (3) These "Songs of the Compassion of Christ," by R. Rolle, are from MS. Cambr. D. V. 64, fol. 134-142, published in the " Library of Early English Writers."

(1) LI. 25, 26, in the original, are as follows :

" Lufe thou me, als the wele aw, And fra syn thou the draw."

(2) The original word for " beloved " is " lem-man."

III. i. (a) (b) (c). Devotions for Communion.

All these devotions for Communion are from Lambeth Cod. 546, p. 37. I have omitted the Latin devotions and four prayers " for a good end of life " that follow the devotions. One or two unimportant verbal alterations have been also made for devotional reasons— e.g. in the thanksgiving after Communion. " Welcome, my noble Lord," is in the original " Wel come, my worthy Duke " ; and " Pontiff" has been substituted for "Pape" in the same column.

2. This second short set of devotions consists of extracts from Ashm. MS. 1286, fol. 223, published in " The Lay-Folks Mass-Book," by Canon Simmons.

IV. i. The Beltej.

This metrical creed is from Lambeth MS. 853. p.39, published by the "Early EnglishText Society," in " Hymns to the Virgin and to Christ." It is preceded by the well-known phrase beginning " Memento homo . . ." used in the distribution of ashes on Ash Wednesday, and by two short Latin epigrams.

Stanzas 11 and 12 refer to the truth that an act of perfect contrition removes the guilt of sin immediately, if the sacrament of penance cannot be had.

IV. 2. Hymn to the Blessed Trinity and our Lady.

This hymn, probably by R. Rolle, is from MS. Thornton, published in the " Library of Early English Writers."

Stanza 2 in the original is omitted. It is difficult to render well in modern English, and is unnecessary to the symmetry of the whole. It runs as follows : " Lorde, hafe mercy of my syne And brynge me ovvte of all my care ; Euylle to doo I couthe neure blyne, I hafe ay wroghte agaynes thi lave ; Thou rewe one me, bathe owte and In, And hele me of my woundes sare." And MS. Vernon, which also contains the poem, adds :

" Lord that at this world schal winne, Hele me ar i fonde and fare."

IV. 3. An Intercession to Jews. This prayer, probably by R. Rolle, is from MS. Thornton, in the " Library of Early English Writers." The original begins as follows :

" Lorde god alweldande I be-tache to-daye in to thi hande My saule & my body, And all my ffrendes specyally, Bathe the quik and the dede : Graunt them parte of my bede."

IV. 4. Two Commendations jor Death.

(i.) From "The Processional of the Nuns of Chester," edited by Dr. Wickham Legg, for the Henry Brad-shaw Society.

(ii.) This prayer forms part of a " Visitatio Infirmorum," [" Here begynneth how men that been in heele (= health) schulde visite seeke (= sick) folke "], composed of extracts from S. Augustine and S. Anselm. It is from MS. Univ. Coll. 97, published in the " Library of Early English Writers," and has been wrongly attributed to R. Rolle. The authorship is unknown. The sick man, looking upon a cross or an image, is to remind himself that it is not God, but " ymaad aftir hym, to make men have the moore mynde of hym after whom (it is) ymagid," and then he is to say the prayer that follows. He is first, however, if it is possible, to be exhorted not to complain, but to welcome death as the " end of alle wykkednesses," and then to be examined in his faith.

IV. 5, The Day of Doom.

This poem, from MS. Rawl. c. 285, published in the " Library of Early English Writers," is of unknown authorship.

Line 11 in the original is as follows:

" The day of crynge & dulfull dyne : The day of bale that neuer sal blyne."

IV. 6. An Epigram.

This epigram, of unknown authorship, is from MS. Reg. I;B XVII., published in the " Library of Early English Writers." At the side is written : Quod bontim est tenete (=»"Hold fast that which is good").

Notes]

IV. 7. Thanksgivings.

(i). To the Blessed Trinity, Possibly by R. Rolle ; from MS. Thornton ; in the " Library of Early English Writers."

Line 2 runs in the original :

" Inewardly I thanke thee."

(2). 7o Jesus. Possibly by R. Rolle : from MS. Thornton ; in the "Library of Early English Writers." Ls. 5, 6, run in the original :

" And my body, swa made of vile matere Thow knyttide to-gedire in Joyntes sere."

IV. 8. A Prayer of the Five Joys and of the Five Sorrows of our Lady.

This prayer, possibly by R. Rolle, is from MS. Thornton, published in the " Library of Early English Writers." The illustration of the light coming through glass without breaking or staining it, is an old image of the mystery of the Virgin-Birth of our Lord.

IV. 9. A Song to Mary.

These verses are from Lambeth MS. 853, pub lished in " Hymns to the Virgin and Christ," by the " Early English Text Society." The Latin lines at the end of the verses together make up the antiphon in the York bidding-prayer. The third stanza is omitted from the original, on account of 214

[Notes

the difficulties of rendering it in modern verse. It runs as follows :

" Heil crowned queene, fariest of alle

Heil that alle our blis in bradde !

Heil that alle wommen on doon calle.

In temynge whanne thei ben hard bistadde !

Heil thou that alle feendis dredde,

And schulen do til the day of doome !

With maidens mylk thi sone thou fedde,

O maria,Jlos virginum."

IV. i o. Devotions to the Guardian Angel.

(i). From Wynkyn de Worde's edition of R. Rolle's works, 1506 ; published in the "Library of Early English Writers."

(2). From the " Processional of the Nuns of Chester" ; edited by Dr. Wickham Legg, for the Henry Bradshaw Society.

IV. ii. Of the Abbey of Saint Spirit.

This allegorical spiritual treatise is attributed in MS. Lamb. 432 to R. Rolle ; but the authorship is uncertain. The text followed here is that of MS. Thornton, published in the "Library of Early English Writers." A sequel, " The Charter of the Abbey of the Holy Ghost," has been added by another author. Several other MSS. contain the treatise, so that we may conjecture it was once popular among the devout.

grtjort !.tfc ef litrfjarb HoIle, tije of

IT is pleasant to think that what is generally known as the " history " of the fourteenth century is only the record of a very superficial part of it. While kings and prelates wrangled, and priests poached in their bishops' preserves, and men in general murdered and mutilated ; yet, beneath all that recorded stir, quiet souls rested in the arms of their Saviour, and ardent souls languished and aspired towards His burning heart, and wept at His streaming wounds ; in prayer and sacrament men and women, at least as much then as in our polished days, found a peace such as the struggling world could neither have not give, and counted it an easy thing to give up all for which the world labours, if they might win that peace and the love of Him from whom it flows. Among these, besides those living in communities such as are, by God's grace, familiar to us in England, there must be counted the anchoret

and the hermit. There was a difference between these. The anchoret (or anchoress) lived in an enclosed cell which he never left. This cell was generally built on to the church, with at least two windows, one looking on to the altar, so that the inmate might assist at the holy sacrifice, while the other was used for interviews with visitors. Thus the anchoret, though enclosed, was far from being without human society. But the hermit was confined to no limited space. He was more of a solitary, but less of a prisoner. Though his vocation, then, was recognised by authority, and he himself set apart by a habit and a cell, yet he was less formal and regular in his life than the anchoret. Neither was under religious obedience, but the hermit was usually free even from any vow, except in the intention of his own soul. They both devoted themselves wholly to the direct praise and glory of God, but the anchoret sang, as a cage bird might, confined within bars, through which men might look ; the hermit as a soaring lark, free but lonely. This exterior silence and solitude, however, were not altogether essential to the hermit's life, and might, if circumstances demanded, be relaxed. It is impossible to exaggerate the significance of such lives, and the effect that they must have had upon the

world of their day. First, it would need an atmosphere of intense faith to produce such lives at all; then there must be reckoned the actual and objective spiritual power generated by these persons' lives, whose business was prayer (as the business of others might be digging or building); lastly, there would be the moral effect produced in the minds of those who saw such lives in their midst. The fact that the single occupation or prayer appears idle or grotesque, or at the best mistaken, to men of our day, is but one more sign of how spiritual faculties are beginning to decay, and becoming less and less capable of appreciating the higher reality of the realm of spirit over the realm of sense, and of understanding that the latter is only of permanent value so far as it is in significant or effectual relations with the former.

Richard Rolle, the hermit of Hampole, from whose writings the greater part of the devotions in this book is drawn, was born at least sometime before the year 1300 A.D., at Thornton Dale, near Pickering, and was educated at Oxford, devoting his particular attention to the study of divinity. When about nineteen years of age he became impressed with thoughts of the solemnity of life and eternity, and determined to give himself

entirely to God. He returned home from Oxford, begged from his sister two of her kirtles and a hood of his father's, adapted them for his own purposes, and dressed himself in them as in a hermit's habit. His sister, when she saw him, cried out in terror that he had gone mad, and he, fearing that his intention would be hindered by the family, quickly withdrew from the house and neighbourhood.

On the vigil of the Assumption he came to a church that seems to have been at Topcliffe to hear evensong, and sat down in the squire's seat, whose name was John of Dalton, and who was a friend of his father's. Lady Dalton, on entering the church, would not allow her servants to disturb him when they wished to make him give place to her. Her sons, too, who had been at Oxford with him, recognised him, and told their mother who he was. On the following day he assisted, without invitation, in the choir at mass, and then, with the leave and blessing of the priest, preached a sermon that moved many to tears. After mass he was with difficulty persuaded to dine with John of Dalton ; he remained silent throughout dinner, and tried to withdraw before the end ; but after a conversation when the meal was ended, he was forced to confess who he was,

though in fear that his father's friend would hinder a vocation contrary to the wish of his family. But John recognised his holy purpose, and himself provided him with a proper habit, a cell on his estate, and daily provision.

Here, then, at Topcliffe, this youth "of at tractive appearance," of a kind to "draw eyes towards him," and "endowed with eloquence," began a kind of solitary novitiate, and soon made great progress in the spiritual life. His writings, even more than his biography, indicate the heights of contemplation to which he rose. He spent nearly three years in purgative and illuminative exercises, in fasting and watching, persevering in "sobbings and sighings," always keeping his mind fixed " in heaven, desiring to be dissolved and to be with Christ, his most sweet beloved/ During this time of probation, he relates, he was visited by fierce and fiery temptations.

At last the rigour of the conflict with self was over, and he began to rise to pure contemplation. Of his experiences in this high region his writ ings tell us much. There are, he relates, three stages in contemplation as he experienced it, which follow one another at first, and then com bine, like a chord played arpeggio and then held down. These stages, or elements, he names

"Warmth," "Sweetness," "Melody." The Warmth came upon him in contemplation at first at any rate so sensibly that it seemed to be physical; combined with this was Sweetness. Then after nine months the Melody came to him. He first heard it, as it were, externally and from above, and then it entered in and remained with him, turning all his thoughts to music and his words to rhythm. This great gift, he says, is granted only to those who especially love the holy name of Jesus. In this connection it is worth recalling the instance of S. Francis of Assisi, who used to pretend fancifully to accompany, on a piece of wood used as a fiddle, the ideal music that flooded his soul; and, indeed, to remember too that a passionate devotion to music is, as M. Joly points out in his study or the psychology of the saints, a frequent characteristic of the saintly lire.

These three stages, it will be seen, correspond to the three senses of Feeling, Taste, and Hearing. It is a well-known principle of spiritual exercises, notably in those of S. Ignatius Loyola, that the senses should be employed in the assimilation of divine truth. And it is of interest, too, to notice that in the " Revelations of Divine Love " given to Mother Julian of Norwich, an anchoress of

the fifteenth century, nearly all comes to her through the medium of Sight, with audible expla nations in connected sentences. But this latter mystic was unlettered, and therefore would pro bably be unable to describe to others any percep tions of truth given to her that were not actually visible or articulate ; while it would require an educated mind, such as was Richard's, to convey to others any sense of the significance of Warmth, Sweetness, or Melody. It is interesting, too, to remark how Walter Hilton, who died fifty years after Richard Rolle, and who is sure to have had some acquaintance at least with Richard's writings, in his "Scale of Perfection " gives advice as to how these heavenly visitations that approach the soul through the senses may be distinguished from their diabolical counterfeits.

Above all, however, Richard is a lover. Jesus is to him the one passion ; it is for love of his Lord that he has sought solitude ; for " in solitude Christ speaks to the heart, as a modest lover who embraces not his beloved before all the world." Here the hermit " sits apart from the noise, but glorying in Christ ; he burns and loves; he rejoices and is glad ; wounded with charity, melted by love, he sings a love-song to his beloved, filled with the softest sweetness." 223

"The special gift," he says, "of those that lead solitary life is for to love Jesu Christ"; and all his advance in holiness is gauged by his advance in love. " The diversity of love makes the diversity of holiness and of meed." The contemplative life then, because it is the life of love, " is the most perfect, the most holy, and the most like to the angels, and most full, moreover, of heavenly sweetness, which I think any mortal man is able to grasp." The solitary, then, is not to be pitied. " He hath such sweetness in his mind as the angels have in heaven, though perhaps not so much."

The Life proceeds to describe miracles that were granted him, such as the putting to flight of demons from a death-bed (possibly that of Lady Dalton), and his power of continuing to write his spiritual treatises at the same time that he was actually talking to and advising persons who came to him for guidance.

Soon after his attainment to contemplation he began to travel about; among other places iae visited Anderby, in the diocese of York, where he relieved the bodily sufferings of an anchoress named Margaret, a spiritual friend of his. This travelling about, which he deliberately undertook for the purpose of helping other souls by mixing 224

with them as an equal, was an occasion for many slanders and accusations of worldliness, and even of vice, brought against him, it need hardly be said, without the smallest foundation. These slanders, moreover, made mischief in his friendships, and more than once caused him to leave those who were giving him shelter and food. Yet in his troubles he looked to God alone. " In this dwelling," he writes, "I sought not dignity among men, not human honour, not the praise of lips, not the glory of miracles, not high eminence ; but I yearned to serve God with love of His deity; I longed after Christ, and for this I greedily stretched forth my mind, aspiring unceasingly towards the Author, that I might most ardently embrace the love of the Most High." In all his sorrows and physical pains and discomforts he was divinely consoled. " The Eternal Ruler sent into me a marvellous melody, and although I was in terrible pain, and was sorely troubled with unbearable giddiness, yet so abundantly was I allured and lifted up with unceasing solace, that I always remained as if I were well, however sick I might be."

Finally, after his wanderings, he came to Hampole, where he became spiritual adviser to a Cistercian nunnery.

225 P

Hampole is still a tiny hamlet, about seven miles distant from Doncaster. There has never been a parish church there, and in Richard's time the spiritual needs of the people would no doubt be met by the convent chapel. Of the nunnery there are now no certain traces, except where a few mounds in the meadows by the stream below the hamlet mark its foundations, and beyond a few of its stones built into the school-house. The few grey stone houses nestle together on the steep slope in a shallow nook in the hill, round an open space where the old village spring still runs. There is no trace of Richard's cell; but, in spite of the railway line in the valley, the place has a curious detached air, lying, as it does, a complete and self-contained whole, below the Doncaster road, fringed and shadowed by trees, and bordered with low-lying meadows rich, in early summer, with daisies and buttercups, and dotted with numerous may-trees ; the farthest horizon from the hamlet is not more than a mile or two away.

Here, then, in this quiet retreat he continued his exuberant writings ; and it is to this period of his life that his more sober and restrained works must be attributed ; and here, above all, in the kindly air and tender beauty of the country, he mellowed and perfected his rich gifts of prayer 226

and desire. And at last here he died, in the year 1349 A.D., most probably of the Black Death that raged in the North at this time.

Soon after his death miracles were reported to have been wrought through his relics and by the aid of his intercessions, and pilgrimages began to take place. So great was his reputation that an Office was composed for him in view of his probable canonisation; but ultimately this did not take place. He had many imitators of his way of life, and a crowd of hermits, some reputable and some otherwise, sprang into existence through his example.

Such, then, was his life, and the effects of it, so far as they are visible ; but as to the power of his prayers and merits before the Throne of Grace, both before and since the passing of his soul, who can speak ?

THE END

Printed in Great Britain
by Amazon